STRAIGHT GUYS

STRAIGHT GUYS

GAY EROTIC FANTASIES

Foreword by
Shane Allison

CLEiS
PRESS

Published in the United States by Cleis Press Inc., 2246 Sixth Street, Berkeley, California 94710.

Printed in the United States.
Cover design: Scott Idleman/Blink
Cover photograph: Caroline von Tuempling/Getty Images
Text design: Frank Wiedemann
First Edition.
10 9 8 7 6 5 4 3 2 1

Trade paper ISBN: 978-1-57344-816-1
E-book ISBN: 978-1-57344-830-7

Contents

INTRODUCTION: STRAIGHT TRADE

I had just gotten off work when I heard the phone in my front pants pocket go off. I pulled it out to see who it was calling me at 1:00 o'clock in the morning. It was a text message. I instantly recognized the number. It was Claude, and I was pretty sure I knew what he wanted. *Come over and suck my dick,* it read. I was tired and hungry, but his text message got me a little horned up. I told him I was just getting off work. *Come over. My lady's at the club with her girlfriends. She won't be back until late.* The thought of Claude naked sealed the deal. "Fuck it," I said to myself. I told him I was on my way. I wasn't that far from his apartment. It didn't take me long to get to Claude's place. I tugged at my dick as I got out of the car. I get off on the mystery of sneaking around. My heart was racing like crazy. I trudged up the steep steps that lead up to his apartment. *It's finally happening,* I thought, *we're finally going to do this.* I tapped gently on the door. Claude soon answered wearing nothing but a pair of boxers. It was on.

What is it about straight men that turns us on so much? Perhaps it's the joy of bending that hypocritical hetero majority over on all fours and having our way. As a gay man I have had more than my fair share of some hot straight trade, planting doubt if not dick into their tits-and-ass way of thinking. It makes me wonder if straight and gay still exist, or if they're just another label we all feel the need to use in order to keep our identities intact. Just goes to show nothing is ever simply black and white. And as I scavenge through online personal ads, snagging on the occasional str8-guy sex manifesto, I see proof that these boys aren't afraid to bend the line when the mood suits.

But let me step off my political soapbox here. This ain't one of those kind of books. It's my own experiences that moved this book from idea to the hot page-turner you hold in your hands. From my dirty mind to yours, I have gathered together some of the top scribes in the genre who share similar appetites for straight-guy meat—like Rob Rosen, who gets the loins stirring in his new naughty creation, "Gray Area." Find out what happens when two muscle-bound married footballers get it on in Bear-muffin's "Football Fuckbuddies." Mark Wildyr had me when I read the first line in his story, "Deer," which reads, *I've fucked more straights than any other queer I know.* You don't want to miss a word of what happens next. A black-metal groupie gets more than he bargained for in Zeke Mangold's "Metal Head." D. Fostalove hits all the pleasure points in "Pistol Whipped." Nick has the hots for his girlfriend's brother in Bob Vickery's "Family Affair." Jeff Mann returns with beautiful erotic lyricism in his Southern lust-fest, "Redneck Revision." A married innkeeper and his newly single gay guest set the flames burning white-hot under the sheets in Hank Edward's dick-stroking, "Ted and Breakfast." Jeff Funk wants us to know what happens "When

Married Men Come in Cars." You will want to keep one hand free while reading Gregory L. Norris's "Taxicab Confession." Garland Cheffield has the remedy for those straight men we lust after the most in "The Lust Lure." Find out what happens in Barry Lowe's "Window of Opportunity." No one can hear you moan with ecstasy when you're "High in the Salt Wind" in Nick Arthur's sexy romp. Jamie Freeman continues to prove to us that cityscapes are not the only places in which hot sex happens when he takes us way down South to Jacksonville, Florida, circa 1952, with "Epiphany," and R. Talent brings things to a fever pitch in "Daddy Mack." I hope you enjoy reading the stories as much as I did, and it's okay if you can't keep it in your pants while you do.

I would like to thank the writers collected in these pages, without whose brilliance and creative imaginations this anthology wouldn't have been possible.

Crimson kisses and elephant hugs,

Shane Allison
Tallahassee, Florida

FAMILY AFFAIR

Bob Vickery

Nick and Maria ride up front in Maria's beat-up '74 Buick convertible, Maria driving like a lunatic, weaving in and out of the traffic, me wedged in the backseat with all the beach gear tumbling over me. The radio is turned on full blast, set to an oldies station, belting out a Beach Boys tune. "I wish they all could be California girls," Nick sings along. He buries his face into Maria's neck and makes loud farting noises. Maria screams with laughter, and it's only by the grace of God that she avoids plowing us all into the highway's concrete median.

"Jesus Christ!" I cry out in terror.

Nick and Maria crack up, Nick wheezing, Maria's shoulders shaking spasmodically. "What the hell is wrong with you guys!" I shout. "You been sniffing airplane glue?"

"No," Nick says. "Drano." Maria breaks up again, laughing until she starts hiccuping.

"You two are fucking crazy," I say, shouting over the wind and the radio. "You're going to kill us all."

Nick turns his head and looks at me grinning. "Lighten up, Robbie," he says. "We're supposed to be having a good time." I glare at him. He turns back to Maria. "I didn't know your little brother was such a tight ass," he laughs.

"Oh, Robbie's okay," she says. She glances back at me in the rearview mirror and widens her eyes in comic exaggeration. I turn my head away sulkily and stare over toward the ocean stretching out on my left as flat and shiny as a metal plate.

We ride for a few minutes in silence. Nick reaches over and turns down the radio. He turns his head toward me. "So, Robbie," he says affably. "I hear you're gay."

"Jesus, Maria!" I exclaim.

Maria isn't laughing now. At least she has the decency to look embarrassed. "I didn't think you'd mind me telling him, Robbie," she says. But her guilty tone makes it clear she knew damn well I'd mind. She shoots a poisonous look at Nick. "You've got a big mouth," she hisses.

"He's not the only one," I say.

Nick's eyes shift back and forth between Maria and me. "Oops," he says. He laughs, unfazed. "It's no big deal. I'm cool. It's not like I'm a born-again Christian or anything." He looks at me. "So are you just coming out or what?"

"I don't want to talk about it." Maria flashes me an apologetic glance in the mirror, but I just glower back at her. We ride the rest of the distance to the beach in silence.

It's still early, the sun has just started climbing high and there is only a scattering of cars in the dirt parking lot. We start the trek to the beach, Nick and Maria leading the way, me lagging behind with the cooler. Nick leans over and says something to Maria, and she laughs again, her previous embarrassment all forgotten now, which makes my mood even pissier. At the top of the dunes, the two of them wait for me to catch up. The sea

stretches out before us, sparkling in the bright sun, the waves
hissing as they break upon the sandy beach. "Bitching!" Nick
says. He reaches over and squeezes the back of my neck. "You
having a good time, Robbie?" he asks, smiling. Though I hardly
know the guy, I know that this is as close to an apology as I'll
ever get. A breeze whips over the dunes, smelling of the sea, the
sun beats down benevolently, and I see nothing but good humor
in Nick's wide, blue eyes. In spite of myself, I smile. "Attaboy,"
Nick laughs. "I knew you had it in you!" He lets go and we start
climbing down the dunes to find a stretch of beach isolated from
everyone else.

After we've laid the blanket out, Maria and Nick start taking
off their clothes. I hurry to pull my bathing suit out of my knap-
sack. "I'm going to change behind the dune," I say.

Nick has one leg raised, about to pull off a sneaker. "I'll go
with you," he says abruptly.

I have mixed feelings about this but don't know how I can
dissuade him. We circle the nearest dune, leaving Maria behind
on the broad expanse of beach. Nick peels off his shirt, and
I can't help noticing the sleek leanness of his torso, the blond
dusting of hair that marches across his chest. My throat tightens,
and I turn my attention to my fingers fumbling with the buttons
of my jeans. Nick kicks off his shoes and shucks his shorts and
Calvins. The honey-brown of his skin ends abruptly at his tan
line, and his hips are pale cream. Nick turns his back to me and
stretches lazily, like a jungle cat, arms bent. His ass is smooth
and milky, downed with a light fuzz that gleams gold in the
sun's rays. Nick turns around and smiles at me. His dick, half
hard, sways heavily against his thighs.

I turn away and quickly pull my jeans off. When I look back
at Nick, he's still standing there, naked, only this time his dick
is jutting out fully hard, twitching slightly in the light breeze.

He sees my surprise and shrugs helplessly. "Sorry," he says with a grin, his eyes wide and guileless. "Open air always makes me hard."

"This isn't a nude beach," I say, trying to sound casual. "You have to wear a suit."

"In a minute," Nick says. "I like feeling the breeze on my skin." His smile turns sly, and his eyes lose some of their innocence. He wraps his hand around his dick and strokes it slowly. "You like it, Robbie?" he asks. "Maria calls it my love club."

"What the hell are you trying to prove?" I ask.

Nick affects surprise. "I'm not trying to prove anything," he says, his tone all injured innocence. "I'm just making conversation." I quickly pull on my suit and walk back to the blanket. Nick joins us a couple of minutes later.

Nick and Maria race out into the waves. She pushes him into the path of a crashing breaker, laughing as he comes up sputtering. They horseplay in the surfline for a while and then swim out to deeper water. Eventually they're just specks in the shiny, gun-metal blue. I close my eyes and feel the sun beat down on me. Rivulets of sweat begin to trickle down my torso.

Suddenly I'm in shade. I open my eyes and see Nick standing over me, the sun behind him so that I can't make out his features, just an outline of broad shoulders tapering down. He shakes his head and water spills down on me. "Hey!" I protest.

He sits down beside me on the blanket. "The water feels great," he says. "You should go in."

"In a little while," I say. "Where's Maria?"

Nick gestures vaguely. "Out there somewhere. She didn't want to come in yet." He stretches out next to me, propped up on his elbows. "So why are you so upset about me knowing you're gay? You think I'll disapprove or something?"

"Jeez, what's with you! Will you just drop the subject?"

"I've gotten it on with guys," Nick goes on, as if he hadn't heard me. "It's no big deal." He grins. "You want to hear about the last time I did?"

"No," I lie.

"It was in Hawaii. Oahu to be exact." Nick turns on his side and faces me, his head on his hand. "I was there on Spring Break in my junior year of college. I started hanging out with this dude I'd met in a Waikiki bar, a surfer named Joe." He laughs. "Surfer Joe, just like in the song. Ah, sweet Jesus, was he ever beautiful! Part Polynesian, part Japanese, part German. Smooth brown skin; tight, ripped body; and these fuckin' dark, soulful eyes." He smiles. "Like yours, Robbie. Like Maria's too, for that matter," he adds, as if in an afterthought. "Anyway I had a rented car, and we took a drive to the North Shore. Somehow, we wound up lost on this little piss-ass road, nothing but sugar cane fields on either side. It'd been raining but the sun was just breaking out and all of a sudden, wham! This huge, Technicolor rainbow comes blazing out, right in front of us." Nick sits up, getting excited. "It was fuckin' awesome! The motherfucker just arced overhead like some kind of neon bridge and ended not far off in this little grassy patch beyond the cane. Well, Joe leaps out of the car—I tell you, he was one crazy bastard—and he races across the field toward the rainbow, and, because I can't think of anything better to do, I do the same." Nick's eyes are wide, and he's talking faster now. "Joe makes it to where the rainbow hits the ground, he pulls off his board shorts, and he just stands there naked, his arms stretched out, the colors pouring down on him, blue! green! red! orange! I strip off my shorts too and jump right in." Nick laughs, but his eyes drill into me. "It was the strangest damn sensation, standing in that rainbow, my skin tingling like a low-voltage current was passing through me. Joe wrestles me to the ground, one thing leads to another, and we wind up fucking right there, with all the colors washing over us, me plowing Joe's ass, Joe's head red, his chest orange, his belly yellow, his legs green and blue. When I finally came, I pulled out of Joe's ass, raining my jizz down on him, the drops like colored jewels." Nick gazes down at me, his eyes laughing. "Like I said: fucking awesome!"

"You are so full of shit," I say.

Nick adopts an expression of deep hurt. "It's true. I swear it."

"Fuck you. You can't stand in a rainbow, for Christ sake. It's against the laws of optics."

"'The laws of optics,'" Nick snorts. "What are you, an optician?"

"You mean a physicist. An optician prescribes glasses. Jesus, you're an ignorant fuck."

But Nick refuses to be insulted. He laughs and picks up my tube of sunblock. "Here," he says. "Let me oil you up again. You've sweated off your first layer." Nick smears the goop on my chest and starts stroking my torso. His hand wanders down my belly, and lies there motionless. I can feel the heat of his hand sink into my skin. The tips of his fingers slide under the elastic band of my suit. He looks at me, eyebrows raised. When I don't say anything, Nick slips his hand under my suit and wraps it around my dick. "Do the same to me," he urges.

"Maria..." I say.

Nick scans the ocean. "She's way out there. She can't see anything." His hand, still greased with sunblock, starts sliding up and down my dick. I close my eyes. "Come on," he whispers. "Do it to me too. Please."

My hand seems to have a mind of its own. It slides inside Nick's suit and wraps around his fat, hard dick. His *love club*. "Yeah, Robbie, that's good," Nick sighs. "Now stroke it."

We beat each other off, the sun blasting down on us, the
ocean shimmering off in the distance like a desert mirage.
After a few moments we pull our suits down to our knees. Nick
smears his hand with a fresh batch of lotion and then slides it
down my dick. I groan. "Yeah, baby," he laughs. "You like that,
don't you?" I groan again, more loudly, arching my back as the
orgasm sweeps over me. Nick takes my dick in his mouth and
swallows my load as I pump it down his throat. Even after I'm
done, he keeps sucking on my dick, rolling his tongue around it,
playing with my balls. He replaces my hand with his, and with
a few quick strokes, brings himself to climax, shuddering as his
load splatters against his chest and belly.

Maria staggers out of the surf a few minutes later and races
to the blanket, squealing from the heat of the sand on her soles.
Nick and I are chastely reading our summer novels under the
umbrella. She flings herself down on the blanket, grabs a towel
and vigorously rubs her hair. "You guys enjoying yourselves?"
she asks.

"Yeah, sure," Nick says, his mouth curling up into an easy
grin. "Except your degenerate little brother can't keep his hands
off me." He winks. Maria laughs, but she shoots me a worried
look, checking to see if I'm offended. I shrug and smile back. I
feel like shit.

Nick stops by my place a week later. It's the first time I've
seen him since the beach. "Is Maria here?" he asks. "I swung by
her apartment but she wasn't home." He's dressed in a tank top
and cutoffs, and he carries a summer glow with him that makes
him shine like a small sun.

"No," I say, my heart beating furiously. "I haven't seen her
all day."

Nick peers over my shoulder. "You alone?"

"Yeah," I say. My mouth has suddenly gone desert dry.

Nick regards me calmly, waiting. "You want to come in for a while?"

Nick smiles and gives a slight shrug. "Why not?"

As soon as I close the door behind us, he's on me, pushing me against the wall, his hard dick dry-humping me through the denim of his shorts, his mouth pressed against mine. After the initial shock passes, I kiss him back, thrusting my tongue deep into his mouth. Nick's hands are all over me, pulling at my shirt, undoing the buttons, tugging down my zipper. He slides his hands under my jeans and cups my ass, pulling my crotch against his.

I push him away, gasping. "This isn't going to happen," I say.

Nick looks at me with bright eyes, his face flushed, his expression half annoyed, half amused. "Now, Robbie," he says, smiling his old smile. "You're not going to be a cock-tease, are you?"

I zip my pants up again and rebutton my shirt. I feel the anger rising up in me. "You're such an asshole," I say. I push past him and walk into the living room.

Nick remains in the hallway. I sit on the couch, glaring at him. He slowly walks into the room until he's standing in front of me. He looks out the window and then back at me again. "Why am I an asshole?" he asks. "Because I think you're fuckin' beautiful?"

"You may not give a damn," I say, "but Maria's crazy about you."

Nick sits down beside me on the couch. "Ah," he says quietly. A silence hangs between us. "What if I told you I'm just as crazy about Maria?" he finally asks.

"You have a funny way of showing it."

Nick leans back against the arm of the couch and regards

me with his steady, blue gaze. He gives a low laugh. "Now, next on 'Jerry Springer'!" he says. "My sister's boyfriend is putting the moves on me!" I look at him hostilely, not saying anything. He returns my stare calmly. "You know," he says, "lately, every time I fuck your sister, I think of you. It's getting to be a real problem."

"Will you knock it off?"

Nick acts like he hasn't heard me. "It's no reflection on Maria, believe me. She's a knockout. Great personality, beautiful..." He leaves the sentence hanging in the air, lost in thought. His eyes suddenly focus on me. "But there are things I want that she can't give me."

I wait a while before I finally respond. "What things?"

Nick's smile is uncharacteristically wistful. "You, Robbie. That's 'what things.'" I don't say anything. Nick lays his hand on my knee. "It's amazing how much you look like Maria, sometimes. The same dark eyes, the same mouth, the same way you tilt your head... It's like the excitement of meeting Maria all over again." He leans forward, his eyes bright. "Only you have a man's body, Robbie. That's what Maria can't give me." His hand slides up my thigh. "She can't give me a man's muscles, a man's way of walking and talking..." His hand slides up and squeezes my crotch. "A man's dick. I swear to god, if I had the two of you in bed together, I wouldn't ask for another thing for the rest of my motherfuckin' life!" He looks at me and laughs. "You should see your face now, Robbie. You look like you just sucked a lemon."

I feel my throat tightening. "You're crazy if you think that's ever going to happen."

"Maybe I *am* crazy," Nick sighs. His eyes dart up to mine. "But I'm not stupid." His fingers begin rubbing the crotch of my jeans, lazily sliding back and forth. He grins slyly. "If I can't have you and Maria together, I'll settle for you both one at a time." He leans his face close to mine, his hand squeezing my dick. "Come on, Robbie, don't tell me I don't turn you on. Not after our little session on the beach." I don't say anything. Nick's other hand begins lightly stroking my chest, fumbling with the buttons of my shirt. "You want monogamy, Robbie?" he croons softly. "I promise I'll stay true to you and Maria. I'll never look at another family."

"Everything's a joke with you," I say. But I feel my dick twitch as his hand slides under my shirt and squeezes my left nipple.

"No, Robbie," Nick says softly. "Not everything." He cups his hand around the back of my neck and pulls me toward him. I resist, but not enough to break his grip, and we kiss, Nick's tongue pushing apart my lips and thrusting deep inside my mouth. He reaches down and squeezes my dick again. "Hard as the proverbial rock!" he laughs.

"Just shut up," I say. We kiss again, and this time I let Nick unbutton my shirt. His hands slide over my bare chest, tugging at the muscles in my torso. He unbuckles my belt and pulls my zipper down. His hand slides under my briefs and wraps around my dick.

"We're going to do it nice and slow this time," Nick says. He tugs my jeans down, and I lift my hips to help him. It doesn't take long before Nick has pulled off all my clothes. He sits back, his eyes slowly sliding down my body. "So beautiful..." He stands up and shucks off his shirt and shorts, kicking them away. He falls on top of me, his mouth burrowing against my neck, his body stretched out full against mine.

I kiss him again, gently this time, our mouths barely touching. His lips work their way over my face, pressing lightly against my nose, my eyes. His tongue probes into my ear, and his breath sounds like the sea in a conch shell. I feel his lips move across my skin, down my torso. He gently bites each nipple, swirling his tongue around them, sucking on them. I can only see the top of his head, the shock of blond hair, and I reach down and entwine my fingers in it, twisting his head from side to side. Nick sits up, his legs straddling my hips, his thick cock pointing up toward the ceiling. He wraps his hand around both our dicks and squeezes them together tightly. "Feel that, Robbie," he says. "Dick flesh against dick flesh." He begins stroking them, sliding his hand up and down the twin shafts: his pink and fat, mine dark and veined. A drop of precome leaks from his dick, and Nick slicks our dicks up with it. I breathe deeply, and Nick grins.

Nick bends down, and tongues my belly button, his hands sliding under my ass. He lifts my hips up and takes my cock in his mouth, sliding his lips down my shaft, until his nose is pressed against my pubes. He sits motionless like that, my dick fully down his throat, his tongue working against the shaft. Slowly, inch by inch, his lips slide back up to my cockhead. He wraps his hand around my dick and strokes it, as he raises his head and his eyes meet mine; he's laughing. "You like that, Robbie?" he asks. "Does that feel good?"

"Turn around," I say urgently. "Fuck my face while you do that to me."

I don't have to ask Nick twice. He pivots his body around, and his dick thrusts above my face: red, thick, the cockhead pushing out of the foreskin and leaking precome. His balls hang low and heavy, above my mouth, furred with light blond hairs. I raise my head and bathe them with my tongue, and then suck them into my mouth. I roll my tongue around the meaty pouch. "Ah, yeah," Nick groans. I slide my tongue up the shaft of his dick. Nick shifts his position and plunges his dick deep down my throat. He starts pumping his hips, sliding his dick in and out of my mouth as he continues sucking me off. I feel his torso squirm against mine, skin against skin, the warmth of his flesh pouring into my body. Nick takes my dick out of his mouth, and I feel his tongue slide over my balls and burrow into the warmth beneath them. He pulls apart my asscheeks and soon I feel his mouth on my asshole, his tongue lapping against the puckered flesh.

"Damn!" I groan.

Nick alternately blows against and licks my asshole. I arch my back and push up with my hips, giving him greater access. No one has ever done this to me before, and it's fucking driving me wild. Nick comes up for air, and soon I feel his finger pushing against my asshole, and then entering me, knuckle by knuckle. I groan again, louder. Nick looks at me over his shoulder as he finger-fucks me into a slow frenzy. "Yeah, Robbie," he croons. "Just lay there and let me play you. Let's see what songs I can make you sing." He adds another finger inside me and pushes up in a corkscrew twist. I cry out, and Nick laughs.

He climbs off me and reaches for his shorts. "Okay, Robbie," he says. "Enough with the fuckin' foreplay. Let's get this show on the road." He pulls a condom packet and small jar of lube out of his back pocket, and tosses the shorts back onto the floor.

I feel a twinge of irritation. "You had this all planned out, didn't you?"

Nick straddles my torso again, his stiff cock jutting out inches from my face. I trace one blue vein snaking up the shaft. "Let's just say I was open to the possibility," he grins. He unrolls the condom down his prick, his blue eyes never leaving mine. He smears his hand with lube, reaches back, and liberally greases up my asshole. Nick hooks his arms under my knees and hoist my legs up and around his torso. His gaze still boring into me, he slowly impales me.

I push my head back against the cushion, eyes closed. Nick leans forward, fully in. "You okay, baby?" he asks. His eyes are wide and solicitous.

I open my eyes and nod. Slowly, almost imperceptibly, Nick begins pumping his hips, grinding his pelvis against mine. He deepens his thrusts, speeding up the tempo. I reach up and twist his nipples, and Nick grins widely. A wolfish gleam lights up his eyes. He pulls his hips back until his cockhead is just barely in my asshole, and then plunges back in. "Fuckin' A," I groan.

"Fuckin' A is right." He props himself up with his arms and proceeds to fuck me good and hard, his balls slapping heavily against me with each thrust, his eyes boring into mine, his hot breath against my face. I cup my hand around the back of his neck and pull his face down to mine, Frenching him hard as he pounds my ass. Nick leaves his dick fully up my ass, grinding his hips against mine in a slow circle before returning to the old in-and-out. He wraps a hand around my stiff dick and starts beating me off, timing his strokes with each thrust of his hips.

We settle into our rhythm, Nick pounding my ass, his hand sliding up and down my dick as I thrust up to meet him stroke for stroke. There's nothing playful or cocky about Nick now: his breath comes out in ragged gasps through his open mouth, sweat trickles down his face and his eyes burn with the hard, bright light of a man working up to shoot a serious load.

I wrap my arms tight around his body and push up, squeezing my asshole tight around his dick at the same time. I look up at Nick's face and laugh. It's the first time I've ever seen him startled. "Jesus," he gasps. "Did you learn that in college?" I don't say anything, just repeat the motion, squeezing my ass muscles hard as I push up to meet his thrust. Nick's body spasms. He groans loudly. "You ought to talk to Maria," he pants. "She could learn some things from you." The third time I do this pushes Nick over the edge. He groans loudly, and his body trembles violently. He plants his mouth on mine, kissing me hard as he squirts his load into the condom up my ass. I wrap my arms around him in a bear hug, and we thrash around on the couch, finally spilling onto the carpet below, me on top, Nick sprawled with his arms wide out.

After a while he opens his eyes. "Sit on me," he says. "And shoot your load on my face."

I straddle him, dropping my balls into Nick's open mouth. He sucks on them noisily, slurping loudly, as I beat off. Nick reaches up and squeezes my nipple, and that's all it takes for me. I give a deep groan, arching my back as my load splatters in thick drops onto Nick's face, creaming his nose and cheeks, dripping into his open mouth. "Yeah," Nick says, "that's right, baby." When the last spasm passes through me, I bend down and lick Nick's face clean.

I roll over and lie next to Nick on the thick carpet. He slides his arm under me and pulls me to him. I burrow against his body and close my eyes, feeling his chest rise and fall against the side of my head. Without meaning to, I drift off into sleep.

When I wake up, the clock on the mantel says it's almost one in the morning. Nick is gone, but he's covered me with a quilt from my bed. I'm too sleepy to get up, and so I just drift back into sleep again.

Nick, Maria, and I are all sitting on Maria's couch, watching *The Night of the Living Dead* on her TV. Maria sits between us, nestling against Nick. We're at the scene where the little girl has turned into a ghoul and is nibbling on her mother's arm like it was a hoagie sandwich. "Gross!" says Maria.

Nick grins. "You're so damn judgmental, Maria," he says. "I

don't put you down when you eat those Spam and mayonnaise sandwiches of yours."

Maria laughs and burrows deeper against Nick. We continue watching the movie. I feel Nick's fingers playing with my hair, and I brush them away with a brusque jerk that I make sure Maria doesn't notice. After a while, though, he's doing it again. When I don't do anything this time, Nick entwines his fingers in my hair and tugs gently. From where she's sitting, Maria can't see any of this. The ghouls are surrounding the farmhouse, now, closing in on the victims inside. Eventually, I lean back and sink into the feel of Nick's fingers in my hair.

REDNECK REVISION

Jeff Mann

For Cindy

I spend late afternoon by the pool. I try to read, but it's impossible to focus. His bare chest's a maddening distraction. It's hard not to stare.

That's as decent a beginning as any. For over two decades I've held on to this memory, regretted never touching him. Now I'm trying to start a short story to rewrite that remembrance, to solidify one of my long-cherished sex fantasies, to reduce the distance between what was and what might have been.

The story's deadline is mid-November. I have about three weeks. But I'm distracted this gray day in October 2010, as I try to remember him clearly, to fictionalize what happened so many years ago. I putter in order to put off writing. I make more coffee. I respond to email. I prepare butternut squash soup for my husbear John's lunch. I do research of a sort, digging through old journals to confirm what I recall. Which summer was it? It takes me a long time to find the journal entry I need.

This spiral notebook: *July 1987–July 1988* says the cover. Yes, here it is, "Lexington Glimpse," a poem I wrote August 20, 1987. Just as I remember: the Holiday Inn. My friend Cindy and I stop there near the end of a trip through Virginia. We get the last available room; we spend the afternoon by the nearly empty pool. And here he is: *motel employee, made to order, / bare-chested, baring a thick crucifix / of black fur, the dark beard of dreams, / old jeans, scuffed boots, moving / from room to room...* It's unusual to see a thirtysomething man servicing motel rooms, rather than the women usually employed for such jobs. It's even more unusual to see Holiday Inn staff in such an informal state of undress.

I'm fascinated, stealing furtive glances. The tough blue-collar look, the long-legged country-boy stride: he's stepped right out of my fantasy life, the smoldering epitome of my type. His beauty's abrasive, aggravating my hopelessness. I'm twenty-eight—perpetually horny, perpetually single. My love life's been nonexistent for years. The men I want never seem to notice me, and I'm far too shy to approach them. This man's my ideal, a sex god. He's fine enough to star in porn. He's a half-naked wonder, only yards away, pushing his cart of sheets and towels. It's a kind of agony, wanting him this badly but in no position to make a move.

Cindy's a lesbian, but she studies him too, as I growl beneath my breath with frustrated lust. He can feel our attention and gives us more than one curious look. Cindy and I joke about the irony of it, what he must think. I'm butch, dark-bearded, solidly built, resembling a younger version of my would-be prey. The guy probably assumes we're straight, thinks that Cindy's lusting after him, that I, her apparent boyfriend, am jealous. If he only knew. *How facades, so laboriously built, often / betray us,* says my journal. *Why are we gifted such glimpses? No hope / for consummation, for compatibility.* He's likely to be a breeder, like most small-town Southern men; he no doubt has a vacuous blonde wife at home and a passel of brats. *I recognize redneck, homophobe, misogynist,* I write. What sweeping assumptions, what grand dismissals. I'm too young to have yet come to terms with my own Southern small-town roots, my own inner redneck, all he and I might have in common. *Fear of disease, rejection, low-life outrage, compromised dignity,* I write, solid excuses not to act. Most of the men I want I fear.

So my redneck sex-god gives us a last glance and finishes his chores. His shift ends; I never see him again. That evening, Cindy and I have an unremembered dinner. That night, I lie in my motel bed, waiting till Cindy's breath shifts into sleep. Feverish with fetish, I tie him up, gag him, suck him off; he ties me up, gags me, rides me hard. Imagining a richer, revised reality, I spill seed into my hand. I remember him for twenty-three years. Today, I hold him, take him in, write him down again.

I spend late afternoon by the pool. I try to read, but it's impossible to focus. His bare chest's a maddening distraction. It's hard not to stare. The thick beard, the tight muscles, the cross-shaped spread of fur across his torso—God might as well have made him for me.

August in Virginia: it's humid and sunny. Cumulus sifts over, edged with gold. I'm the only motel guest around, enjoying the quiet, soaking up the sun, cooling down in the water when I get too sweaty. He's the only motel employee in sight. Thick eyebrows, angular cheeks, square jaw, black hair falling over his forehead—his handsome face is stern, unsmiling, but he gives me a tight little nod every time he pushes his towel-heaped cart past me and once in a while his dark eyes shoot me a hard look.

I hope he likes what he sees. I'm oiled up, sprawled in a lounge chair in my black swim-trunks. I'm six feet tall, about his height. I have a decent build, thanks to the gym: little muscles along my arms, prominent pecs, a dusting of fur over my chest and the crest of my belly, thicker on my thighs and calves. My beard's dark brown; my shaggy hair's tied back. Sunglasses and the WVU baseball cap cocked over my brow allow me to study him without being obvious. The guy looks like the type who'd beat me up if he knew what I was thinking, but that's usually the kind of man I want.

That evening, I'm in my room, finishing off my first Bud Light, wondering where I can fetch some fast food. There's a sharp knock at the door. I open it, dressed in nothing but camo shorts, beer can in hand. It's him, the guy I quietly drooled over all afternoon. He's still shirtless, silhouetted against lavender sky. Under his arm, he's carrying towels. In his other hand, he's holding a gym bag.

He looks me up and down. The stern look fades. Here's his grin, crooked and gentle, framed by that thick black beard. "You need more towels, son?"

Son? Country-bred guys talk like that. I should know. Despite my education, I am one. "Uhhh..." I've never been eloquent around men this hot. I step back, automatically polite, and usher him in. "Uh, sure, sir. Thanks."

In he strides. He puts the gym bag and towels on the dresser. Turning, he looks me up and down again. "You got another one of those?"

"I, uh, what?" I'm standing in the open doorway. A warm breeze tickles my armpits. His chest hair's so thick I can barely make out the hard pink points of his nipples.

"Beer, bud. Beer." He chuckles. "This here's my last room to check. Shift's done now. Feel like a cool drink. Can you spare one or two?" His voice is a deep baritone. His thick accent makes me feel at home.

I shut the door. "Yes, sir, sure." My cock's swelling in my shorts, yes, but inside my chest something else is swelling. Hope, I guess. I'm still young, but I won't be young for long. Celibacy is a sad waste of youth. I haven't been this close to a man this hot in years. So I try to act calm. Don't want to spook him. I fetch him a beer, offer him the armchair and stretch out on the bed.

I'm nervous and shy, but he's a talker, so that makes it easier. By the end of my second beer, I've got a buzz on, and we've both learned a lot.

His name's Bo. He lives just over the mountain, in a trailer in the woods above Goshen. He works at the Holiday Inn part-time, as an auto mechanic part-time. He's divorced and single. Every now and then he drives up the road to the nearest titty bar to see the women dance. He reminds me of the rough-looking rednecks I grew up around back home in Summers County.

My name's Jeff. I teach freshman comp at West Virginia University during the school year but have the summer off. I'm in Lexington in order to do some research for a novel I'm writing, one set during the Civil War. Lee's buried here. Jackson's buried here. The town's a Rebel shrine.

Sun's set, room's dim, beer's done. We crumple cans and toss them in the trash. We share a makeshift dinner: a couple bags of fried pork skins Bo's brought. "Could have won if Jackson hadn't died," Bo says, pouring bourbon from the flask he's fetched from his gym bag. He hands me a glassful, moves to the window and draws the drapes, then tugs off his boots and sits back in the chair. "Gettysburg would've had a different end, you can be damn sure of it, if Jackson was there."

It's hot in here; the air conditioner isn't working well. He pulls a rag from the back pocket of his jeans, using it to wipe sweat off his face, pecs and pits. I can smell him. It's a grassy aroma, like a sun-warm pasture, the patient labor of animals. It makes me even harder than I already am.

We're refighting the war, battle by battle, side by side. He's gotten to the siege of Petersburg when abruptly he stops. He refills his glass. "You queer, kid?" he says into the dark, voice steady and soft.

I'm scared. I lower my eyes. I consider lying.

"You were watching me all damn day. I could feel it."

His gentle tone gives me courage. I take a burning swig, turn on the bedside lamp and look him in the eyes. "Yes, sir. I am," I say as steadily as I can.

Bo gives me a blurry smile. "Thought so." He spreads his legs, unzips his jeans and pulls out his penis. It's half hard, uncut. He strokes it. "You're pretty manly for a cocksucker. You do suck cock, don't you, son?"

I swallow the last of my drink and sit up. "Yes, sir. I do. Pretty good at it too, if you don't mind me saying so. Uh, you negative?" I have to ask.

"Yep. I'm clean. You?"

"Yes, sir."

He's full-on hard now, and his cock's scary, it's so big. Thick, a good nine inches, larger than anything I've handled before. "You wanna suck this?"

"Wow," I say, staring. "Uh, you *bet*." I drop to my knees before him and lick my lips. "*Damn*, you're huge. Take it easy, okay? Don't need a dislocated jaw."

I lick Bo's cockhead; he sighs, grasping the back of my neck. He thrusts into my mouth, gently, not too deep; I get a good rhythm going. His crotch smells great, the perfect mixture of man-musk and soap. His cock is salty and sweet.

"Been a while," he groans. "Feels real fine." He pokes the

back of my throat till I choke. I catch my breath, wipe drool from my chin and start sucking again.

"Hey, hey," he says. "Don't wanna come yet." Gripping my ponytail, he pulls me off. "Get on these tits some." He pushes my face into his chest hair. Eagerly, I tongue-hunt for his nipples, make love to one, then the other. "Down," he says, tugging my hair, and again my mouth's stuffed full of dick.

He's panting, pretty close to coming, and I've got my own cock out, jacking it, when he pushes me off him so hard I fall back onto my butt. "Sorry, kid," he says, rising to his feet. He grabs my hand, helps me up, then suddenly shoves me back onto the bed.

"I wanna fuck you," Bo says. "Bet your little butt's nice and tight."

"Don't think so, man. I haven't been screwed in years, and, well, you're just too damn—"

He's on top of me before I know it. Seizing my wrists, he forces me down.

His grin's turned wicked; there's fire in his eyes. "I thought hot little fags like you would take any dick, any way, any time."

"Not this fag, friend." Got to admit his weight feels great on top of me, but all that Civil War talk has my dander up. I'm feeling like a warrior. "You want a fight?"

"Yep." Bo's voice is a gruff growl. "Loser gets it up the ass. Agreed?"

"Maybe." I wrap a leg around his waist, heave and flip him off. So the battle begins.

He's bulkier than I, stronger than I thought. I thrash and strain against him as best I can, but it only takes him a few minutes to get me on my belly and to twist my right arm behind me.

"Rockbridge County High School wrestling champ, 1967.

Forgot to mention that," Bo hisses in my ear. "Yield!"

When I put up more struggle, he wrenches my arm hard. Pain shoots through my shoulder.

"*Stop*, man. That hurts!"

"I get to fuck you?" Bo wrenches my arm again.

"*No*. Goddamn it, let me go! Get *off* me!"

There's a funny little sound, a click. Something thin and cold's pressed to my throat.

"My first pocketknife. Whittled many a twig. Sharpened this morning. You behave now."

My stomach clenches and my balls constrict.

"You gonna keep still and be quiet?"

The blade slides along my windpipe, touch of a chilly feather.

"Yeah, man, yeah." I swallow hard and go limp. Sweat pops up on my brow. I'm close to pissing myself. And I thought I was a warrior.

"Up." Bo jerks me to my feet, pushes me across the room, bends me over the dresser, pulls my arms behind me. His grasp's like a vise about my wrists. "Stay like that, or I'll cut you."

The sound of a zipper. His jeans? No, as he grips my wrists with one hand, he's searching his gym bag with the other. "Here we go," he says. Rope's looped around my crossed wrists, rapidly tightened and knotted. More about my elbows. More around my upper arms and chest. In only a few minutes, Bo has me trussed up tight. He pulls me upright, shoves me back across the room and onto the bed. A few minutes more, and my shorts are torn off, my ankles crossed and tied. From the gym bag, he fetches a roll of duct tape. He rips off long strips. Wherever he's roped me, now he tapes me up.

"No way you're gonna get out of that," Bo snickers. Rolling me onto my back, he straddles my hips. Gazing down at me with what could be a father's fondness, he strokes my chest. "You ain't going nowhere."

I want to cry, but I mustn't. I want to yell for help, but I'm pretty sure he'll cut me if I do. So instead I say, in a wobbly rasp just this side of a whimper, "God, man, don't hurt me."

"Shut up, kid." From his jeans pocket, he fetches the sweat-rag. He balls it up and stuffs it in my mouth. The cloth tastes and smells great, still damp from his body, but at this point I'm too scared to be turned on. He fastens the rag in place with rope tied between my teeth and around my head, then more tape plastered over my mouth. I should have shouted for help while I could. Too damn late now.

"Done," Bo says, smoothing the tape over my lips. "You look mighty fine. How's that feel?"

I lie there trembling, staring up at him, trying to catch my breath. I've never been so afraid.

"Answer me, son. Does that feel good?" Bo gives my cheek a light slap.

I don't want to piss him off, but I shake my head anyway. "Umm um," is all my cloth-packed mouth can manage.

Bo grins that same crooked, gentle grin. "Would it feel better if I told you that I sure as shit was not gonna hurt you? I just want to have me some fun. The knife's just for show, I swear. Just for the scene. Thought you looked like a tough little guy, thought you might like some rough stuff. I ain't wrong, am I? What if I gave you my word as, well, a fellow son of the South? That I ain't gonna hurt you? I just really, well..."

Bo gets off me. He sits on the edge of the bed and stares at the wall.

"I just really..." Bo clicks off the bedside lamp and lies down beside me. He pulls me into his arms, my face against his chest.

"Ah, poor guy. You're shaking! Relax!" His touch is so tender, fingertips tracing my shoulder blades. He touches me as if he's known me and loved me for years. "You're safe with me. You believe me, right?"

Something in that tenderness, that's what convinces me. "Mmm," I grunt, nodding.

"I need up your ass *real* bad, bud. Been a while since I had me a tight hole. But, well, to be honest, it ain't just that." His fingers comb my beard, fumble loose my bound-back hair. "Been too long since I touched a soul. You can be damn sure I'm gonna rape your butt later, but...right now I just wanna hold you a while. Okay?"

I hesitate, then nod. Under his soft strokes, my cock grows stiff again, my trembling slowly subsides. My body's telling me what my mind hesitates to admit: some part of me has been aching for this, wanting to be mastered by such a man.

Reaching down, Bo grips my dick. "Nice. Damn nice. Hard as hell. So you like this all right, huh?" His lips brush my brow. "Think I found me my bitch." He gives a long sigh, deep with relief.

"Hell, ain't you hot?"

Under the bright light, two men appear in the mirror. One's younger, woven round with rope, with wild hair and wilder eyes, a strip of silver sealing his mouth. The other's older, with a tight smile and glowing, triumphant eyes. One's a slave; one's a god.

With my captor's help, I've hopped on bound feet to the bathroom. My nipples are on fire. After some lengthy snuggling, Bo held me down and chewed them till I teared up and started to sob.

Things go dark as Bo tapes up my eyes. He helps me into the

tub and rolls me onto my belly. He hog-ties me, so tightly my fingers brush my heels. The cold porcelain feels good against my burning chest.

"Lotta beer," says Bo. He pisses for a long time, a warm splashing in my hair, over my back and ass, trickling down my buttcrack. Working a wet finger up inside me, he finds my prostate, finger-fucks me till I'm moaning with bliss.

"Feel good, huh? My dick's going up there soon, whether you like it or not, and that'll feel even better. But now I gotta get home and let the dog out or she'll mess the floor. Be back in an hour or two."

Footsteps, click of the light switch. "I think you know by now I ain't gonna hurt you," Bo says, his voice even gentler than before, "but in case you wanna cry for help, well, the only other folks checked in are on the far side of the motel—a fat couple from Lynchburg, ugly as homemade sin. Out back's nothing but trees. And the night manager tonight, well, that's me. So shout as much as you want. Ain't no one gonna hear you."

Click of the door closing. I lie in Bo's cooling piss. I fight my bonds till the rope cuts into my pecs and biceps, till my wrists and ankles are warm throbs, long enough to know I'm fair and squarely caught. I try to shout, just to see what noise I can muster. Not much more than a ragged grunt.

Hell, why cry for help? I've been looking for a man like Bo all my life.

Another shower of piss wakes me. Then the tape's peeled off my eyes.

"Y'aw right, lil' bitch-boy? Y'aw right?" With the pocket-knife, Bo cuts the rope tethering my ankles to my wrists. It's a relief to stretch out, after so long enduring the tight discomfort of a hog tie.

Bo's real drunk, I can tell. He sits on the toilet lid, drinking from his flask, talking, talking, slurring his words. I lie on my side in a fresh puddle of piss and listen. He tells me about how much he loved his wife, Michelle. How they married right after high school. How he caught her with OxyContin, and then found her splayed out beneath her dealer. Divorced four years ago. How lonely he's been. A couple girlfriends who didn't last, a few anonymous mouths to poke in rest-stop toilet stalls, a hunting buddy who got drunk and sucked Bo off, then never spoke to him again.

Bo falls silent. He drops his flask. He puts his face in his hands and cries, gulping, sniffing, cursing his ex-wife, cursing himself. I want to hold him bad, kiss his wet cheeks, tell him how handsome he is, how sorry I am that he's hurting. All I can do is lie here and watch him cry.

He's done. "Goddammit," he mutters, wiping his eyes with the backs of his hands. "You wan' loose, buddy?"

I mumble an affirmative. Bo frees me. The tape hurts when he peels it off my skin, especially where I'm hairy. He rubs my rope-chafed wrists and stiff limbs, gives my forehead a sloppy kiss. We take a long hot shower. I help him stagger to the bed. "Wanna fuck you but too damn drunk. Sorry, bud, sorry," he mutters, snuggling up against me before he passes out. I think about taking advantage of the situation, turning the tables, raping him the way he plans to rape me. After all, I'm as much Top as I am bottom, and, far as I'm concerned, a man as furry, big-built and butch as he is, that's just the kind of masculine power that looks best tied up and forced to submit. But that's not what Bo needs. Instead, I hold him while he sleeps.

I wake to hands kneading my chest, a hard cock pressed against my ass. I give Bo a little resistance, just so he'll truss me up. Soon enough I'm snugly roped, taped, blindfolded and gagged just as I was before. Bo sits on the bed's edge and pulls me onto his lap. He gives my butt some solid slaps, then spanks me, hard and steady, with his belt. Yawping, I writhe around. He holds me down and beats me harder.

After a while, I stop struggling. "More?" he says. "Bet you can take more."

I nod. Bo continues. He beats me for a long time. I gnaw my gag and fight back tears.

"Nice and red," Bo says, running a hand over my burning butt. "You took a helluva lot. You're a strong dude."

Bo rolls me onto my belly, spreads my burning buttcheeks. "Time for a ride."

Cool lube, the probe of fingers easing me open. Then his cockhead's bumping my hole. He enters me super-slow. It hurts real bad anyway. Feels like my flesh is a fragile fabric being stretched and torn. I shake my head, struggle, beg him to stop. "Easy, easy," he growls, clamping a hand over my mouth. When he pushes past my last resistance, the sharp hurt makes me wince and whimper, but seconds later the painful burn's grading into pleasure. Bo slides farther inside, whispering, "All right, bud? All right? Can you take a little more?" When I nod, he gives me another inch, another, another. Finally he's all the way in, thrusting gently. I've never been filled this full, and man, now it's feeling wonderful.

Once I'm broken in, Bo wraps his arms around me and plows me hard. When he shifts me onto my side, his pounding finds my sweet spot. The rapture mounts and mounts till I'm half wild, bucking against him, shouting into my gag, begging him to fuck me harder, and we're rocking together like high pines in a storm. My captor snarls as he rides me, a string of nastiness that only maddens me more. "Ever been fucked by a dick this big, bitch? Uhhhmmm, your asshole's tight. Tighter than the tightest pussy. Sweet. Fucking sweet. You like this, faggot? You like a fat redneck dick up your butt? Yeah, you love this, don't you, you little pig?" What can I do but nod, moan beneath his hand and squeeze my ass-muscles tighter?

"Here we go," Bo pants into my ear. His hips pump, driving his full length into me. His hand squeezes my dick, I clench my butt, and, gasping, we both pulse out our sticking endings.

I'm sunk inside post-cum drowse, my cock oozing on my thigh, when Bo pulls me back against him. He fondles my belly hair. "Did I hurt you?"

I shake my head. What hurt there was sure turned to heaven fast.

"I'll be wanting me loads more of this." He pats a buttock, fingers my well-fucked hole. "How 'bout you?"

I give an eager grunt, rubbing my rear against his crotch.

"That's what I thought. Look, boy," he says, voice suddenly husky, "how 'bout a little friendly kidnapping? I mean, uh, how 'bout I take you home with me? You have the summer off, right? How 'bout you stick around a while? I sure could use the company." He clears his throat. "I been hoping to meet someone like you, a guy that..."

My answer's instant, a happy nodding.

My captor heaves a sigh. He kisses my shoulder, then swats my butt. "Great! Let's go! I'm sober enough to drive, I swear. We'll pack up your stuff and fetch your vehicle later."

Rustle of Bo dressing. Click of the door as he peers outside.

"Coast's clear," he says. "Ready?"

When I nod, he hoists me up, wraps a steadying arm around me. "Lean on me. Trust me, I ain't gonna let you fall." With his aid, I hop to the door and out into the humid night.

Sound of crickets, warm concrete beneath my bound feet. I sway against him, blind and helpless. Suddenly I'm terrified, and more aroused than I've ever been, to be so vulnerable, so entirely within another man's power.

"No worries," says Bo. "Three a.m. Too early for folks." He helps me hop a few yards more. Jingle of keys, snick of a popped car trunk.

Bo helps me inside. To my surprise, it's lined with soft blankets. "A little nest for my boy-bitch," Bo snickers. "Yeah, I been planning to take you from the beginning." He positions me on my side, slips a pillow beneath my head, covers me with a blanket, tucks me in. "Cozy, son?"

Hell, yes, Dad. I give a vigorous nod.

"Don't you worry now. I'll take real good care of you. We'll be home in half an hour. And I'm thinking, come morning, your tight little ass is gonna need fucked again."

The trunk snaps closed. Boot-heels click on asphalt. The engine turns over. I curl into my warm cocoon as we move forward.

The story has every element of fetish I cherish: beards, body hair, bondage, gags, ass-fucking, abduction. Three times in the writing of it I come in my lounge pants. At this age, writing's one of the few places left I can put my passion.

At night I dream about Bo. This time I'm the Top. He and I are still young, still hot. I tie him up, stuff a rag in his mouth, make love to his nipples and cock for hours, roll him over and rape him. His gagged groans are pure gratitude.

In 1987, he looked about a decade older than I. I'm fifty-one now. Where is he? What happened to him? What kind of life has he led? Is he still alive? Hell, if he is, he's probably lost his looks; he's probably plumper and grayer than I. Here's hoping, at least once, another man sucked or fucked him, or he sucked or fucked another man. Wish that man could have been me.

Might have been if I'd been braver, taken a chance, was less constrained by country manners.

This sunny afternoon, after I finish the first draft, I walk around the lawn. Mid-October's a long, warm pause, before the steep descent into cold, before bleaker facts congregate. The morning glories my husbear planted—white, purple, sapphire— are fading; the sunflowers are burnt out. Tonight will bring the first freeze, so we'll harvest the basil, clip the last white roses, gather in the green tomatoes. Tonight, I'll make coleslaw, fry oysters; we'll split a bottle of wine. John and I always drink and eat really well. Later, we'll watch a bondage video he's down-loaded for me, and we'll jack off side by side. We'll sleep in our big bed, hemmed in by affectionate tabbies. I'll jack off again in the middle of the night, when I can't sleep, when I lie there and regret, when I remember Bo's half-naked body by the pool, his stern bearded face; wishing I could see him again, thank him for the years of fantasy, thank him for being so beautiful.

When I wake, the lawn will be gray with frost. I'll sip coffee, polish and proofread Bo's story and send it off to the editor. I'll return my old journals to their dusty box in the guest bedroom. Then I'll fry some green tomatoes and help John prepare pesto. We'll make the best of what summer's left; we'll mark the final harvest.

DEER

Mark Wildyr

I've fucked more straights than any other queer I know. I've also had more fights. The ultimate high is to make it with a straight arrow after I whip his ass. Don't get me wrong. I'm not into rape. But I've fucked Egyptians, Europeans, Thais, Chinese, Filipinos, Mexicans, Argentines and I don't know how many others. And shit, I'm only thirty.

My name is Byron Ryer, although no one ever calls me Byron more than once. I'm Ryer or Master Sergeant Ryer. In the part of Oklahoma where I grew up, bibles weren't exactly thumped, but they were consulted frequently. Realizing I was a homosexual necessarily transformed me from a mama's boy into a quasi-bully in a few short years.

I was built and better looking than most guys and a little too obsessed with male asses, so figuring the military might put some discipline in my life, I joined up right out of high school. Man, was I wrong. I got more man butt in the Air Force than on the outside, and when they put me through Special Operations

Training, they made me damned near invincible and sent me all over the world in search of new stuff. I never found a country or a continent without a good-looking stud willing to fuck.

At the end of my third tour in 'Stan, I was sent to a Nuclear Bomb Storage outfit at Kirtland Air Force Base at Albuquerque, New Mexico where I became a fucking policeman. All that special training, and I was nothing more than a glorified military security cop. But I'd just made master sergeant, so I hunkered down and made the best of it.

When Airman John Deer appeared on my radar, I knew things would be all right. I had a personal project again. With a name like John Deer, you'd expect him to be built like a tractor, right? Well, he had the fine, taut muscles of a young stag trembling with nervous energy in a fight-or-flight mode. John was assigned to the flight's mailroom and took some classes at the University of New Mexico. He was bright and eager to learn, and I was willing to teach him—just not what he had in mind.

John was the most handsome man I've ever seen. The Egyptian was the most beautiful, as comely as any woman. The Thai was the most exotic, but he thought he was a woman, which was a turn-off. But John Deer, a pure-blood American Indian of about twenty years, was the *handsomest* man of any race, religion or creed I'd come across. He was a changeling, different from day to day. Sometimes his thick black hair glistened like onyx; others, it absorbed the sun's rays like some mysterious black hole.

John's eyes matched his hair, except they gleamed all the time, like they were wet with tears...black and unfathomable. The broad, mobile mouth gave the only clue to the guy's thinking. His ears lay close against his skull, and while ears have never been a turn-on for me, *his* gave me an erection. Go figure. Deer's dark skin was what really set me throbbing. It was smooth and stretched tight over bones and muscle with hair only in the right places. I liked that; the muscles showed clear and clean without any fur to mask their shape.

He played basketball with some of the other airmen during the noon hour, and when he played skins, I made a point of playing shirts so I could guard him. Long, ropy muscles gave him a grace that bordered on the feline. No matter how rough the game, Deer never lost his temper. He had one mood...good-ole-boy, Indian style.

Normally, I would simply have faced him and told him he made me wet my pants. Then he'd either slug me—at which time we'd get it on—or he'd show some interest—at which time we'd get it on. Or he'd look at me like I was crazy and walk away, ending the whole thing. But sexual harassment is a serious charge in the military, and I didn't have the slightest clue if John would be receptive to my approach. Still, I made it a habit to speak whenever he delivered mail to the security office.

I managed to keep everything copacetic until he spoiled things. The knock on the door startled me out of my review of the previous night's security checks.

"Sorry, Sarge, am I interrupting?" The open neck of John's blue blouse invited the eye to his broad chest. The fatigues hugged slim hips as he shifted his weight nervously. Today his hair was in its wet-coal mode.

I waved him inside. "Come on in, Airman. What can I do for you?" The Karen Carpenter song from the stereo on the government-issue credenza behind me faded as if his presence absorbed the noise. This kid could turn a carload of rednecks gay.

"I...I, uh, need some advice."

"Sit down and fire away." My heart rate, and probably my blood pressure, spiked.

He settled his lanky frame in a chair and scowled again.

"I'm working on my degree at the U, and was thinking about taking a class in criminology. I just wondered what you thought about that? You know, you being in security and all."

"Security's not criminology, so I don't know if I can help. But you're bright enough to profit from any class you take. Were you thinking of criminology as a career?"

"No, computer science is my major, but I might make crim my minor." John didn't often look directly at you, but now his big, black eyes rested on me briefly before falling away. So help me, I got hard.

"Might be an interesting combination. Computers are as important to criminologists as they are to everyone else."

"Does it take a special type of person to be a criminologist?" My Air Force–gray office walls seemed to close in on us.

"Well, a fellow ought to be curious and suspicious and have the capacity for a lot of detail work," I said as calmly as I could in my rising state of excitement. "An ability to stick with it when the going gets slow. A good sense of right and wrong wouldn't hurt." John Deer was showing some depth that I hadn't known he possessed. It made him all the more interesting.

"I've got a couple of books at my billet," I went on. "One's on criminology and the other's abnormal psychology. You're welcome to come by and take a look at them."

"I don't have a class tonight or anything," he tested the water.

"I'll be home by eight, if that's not too late for you."

He left after I gave him my address, and the room magically reverted to normal size. The stereo was suddenly too loud. Interest in last night's security report had evaporated, but I summoned enough self-discipline to go over it carefully and then go out to raise hell with a couple of techs, one of the prerogatives of a master sergeant.

The old man called a meeting at the end of the day, and

I fretted through the whole thing, afraid I'd miss Deer. But I was home, showered, shaved, and waiting impatiently by seven-thirty. For a fellow who considers himself unflappable, I was thoroughly shocked when I saw a pretty young woman with him when I opened the door.

"Hi, Sergeant Ryer," he said in that voice that came up out of his belly...or perhaps his balls.

"Come on in, Airman." I stepped aside so they could enter my small foyer.

"This is Cara. She's a friend of mine."

"Nice to meet you, Cara. Are you military, too?"

"No, I'm a secretary in a law office downtown. I met John at a club. Hope that doesn't disqualify me for admission."

"Not at all. I get tired of Air Force blue like everyone else. Rainbows are welcome sometimes. Come in and have a seat. Something to drink?" Mild punk rock leaked out of wall speakers. I lowered the volume as they claimed places on the couch.

"No, thanks, we just had dinner."

"Speak for yourself, Tonto," the girl said. "A glass of white wine if you have some, please." She was short, but with a lot of curves. I read interest in her blue eyes, but that wasn't unusual. Women often found me interesting. And occasionally, I reciprocated.

"Then I'll have a beer." John draped an arm across her shoulders as they relaxed against pale-green velour sofa cushions.

"Nice quarters," John said as I settled into a chair after delivering drinks. "Damned sight better than the enlisted dorm."

I indicated the two books carefully centered on the glass and chrome coffee table. "Well, there they are. I haven't cracked either one of them in a while, but you might find them of interest. Feel free to borrow them." Damn, and I'd hoped we'd spend an hour at the kitchen table reviewing the blessed things.

"Thanks." When he settled back from picking up the books, his leg rode hard against the girl's. I started getting hard again.

They didn't stay long, and the door was hardly closed behind them before I fell to my knees, ripped open my britches and jerked off all over the beige carpet while Elvis wailed a lonely ballad through the speakers. This had to stop. No stud had gotten to me like this since high school.

I purposely avoided Airman Deer all the next week, but just as I was coming to the conclusion avoidance wasn't doing the job, he did me in again.

"Sergeant Ryer?" He rapped on the open door frame after retreat on a Friday night. My consternation must have shown because he backed up a step. "Sorry, I didn't mean to bother you."

I managed a smile. "Come on in. I was just thinking about something." *Yeah, I was thinking about kissing you, you hand-some hunk.* "What's up?"

"Just wanted to return your books and say thanks."

"They help any?" Man, maybe he was prettier than the Egyptian. Fucking beautiful.

"Criminology's got a lot of statistics to it, but I found it interesting."

The walls started their shrinking act. "You read both of them?"

"Yeah. Some parts more carefully than others, but I read them."

"You're a better man than I am, Gunga Din," I quipped. "I barely cracked either one when I took the classes." Despite my resolve of the past three weeks, I didn't want him to go. "Sit down. How's Cara? That's a pretty woman you've got there."

He laughed. "I don't have Cara. Nobody does."

"All's not well in the romance department?"

"What romance? Cara's got goals, I guess you'd say. And they don't include some redskin from the sticks except—" He bit down on his tongue.

"Except for stud service, huh?" My sphincter puckered at the mental image.

He grinned. "Yeah. That's about it."

"So who else is in your stable?"

"Nobody right now. Just doing my job for the Force and going to school to make myself more valuable to Uncle Sam. That's a full plate."

"Are you a career man?"

"Don't know yet. But it's a pretty good life."

That innocent, friendly visit of about fifteen minutes completely did me in. That night, I put on my tightest civvy chinos, sexiest tapered shirt, a pair of high-gloss cowboy boots and beat it out the door. Disdaining the gay bars, I drove directly to a big barn of a country and western place on East Central, a bastion of heterosexual pseudo-cowpunchers and equally fake cow gals. I worked the noisy, cavernous room slowly, pacing my drinks and avoiding the worst of the cigarette smoke. I could have been in a German beer hall cruising for a lonely GI except the music was C&W strings and percussion, not oom-pah-pah brass and percussion.

It was almost midnight before I saw and followed a guy headed for the front door. At first, I thought it was John, but as I caught up to him in the parking lot, he turned out to be a lighter, shorter look-alike with the slight flush of one who's hit the booze too hard. His forehead glistened with a fine sweat that would smell and taste of alcohol. He barely glanced at me as I put a hand on his shoulder. Then he did a double take when he saw a brown-haired, blue-eyed Celt standing beside him. Man, these Indians were either as ugly as sin or as handsome as…well, sin. My old cock stirred.

"'Sup, bro," he slurred.

"Not much." I allowed my eyes to wander his face and form. Slender, corded, tough…and a face like a fallen angel. "Man, I'd sure like to fuck your handsome butt."

The kid's eyes flew open. He'd probably never gotten sober so fast. For a second I regretted destroying the alcoholic cocoon he'd spent the whole night weaving.

"What are ya?" he slung it all together. "Some kinda queer?"

"I'm queer for you." I was hard now. This kid wasn't going to just walk away. One way or the other, I was going to get some action. I ignored his glower. "You're a handsome fucker, you know that? Has a man ever said that to you?"

"Get the fuck away from me, whitebread!"

"I like your shoulders. You're long in the torso. I like that, too. Bet you don't have much body hair. Man, that turns me on. Are you cut?"

"None a your fucking business. You get outa my face and maybe I won't break your nose, cocksucker!"

A little precum leaked into my shorts. "You've got it wrong. I want to fuck you, not suck you. Of course, if that's one of the preliminaries, I—"

"You fag asshole, I'm gonna beat you to a fucking pulp!"

"You can try. But tell me your name so I'll know who I hurt tonight." Little electrical pulses played down my arms, sensitizing my fingertips.

"Lonnie. And I'm gonna make you cry, you dirty shit!"

"Okay, Lonnie. But I don't want you to get into trouble when you whip my candy ass, so let's go someplace where we won't be interrupted. "You got a car?"

"Fucking A, I got wheels, man."

It took some maneuvering, but I cajoled him into following me to a big open field just outside the air base that was usually deserted this time of night. The security lights of some of the base's buildings tucked behind an eight-foot chain-link fence some two hundred yards away provided murky illumination. When the guy barreled out of the cab of his old pickup, he hadn't cooled down a bit.

"Now I got you," he yelled before telegraphing his lunge.

Lonnie was a bar brawler, and a pretty good one at that, but I had been trained by masters. I played with him, indulging my rising sexual excitement, allowing him to expend his energy. He was a drinker, so it didn't take long. Although exhausted, he stubbornly kept up his guard, absorbing my short, sharp jabs on his forearms. Then his shoulders took the punishment. After that, he drooped so badly his chest and stomach were exposed. I ended the thing by stepping in and burying a fist in his belly. As he went down like a wet dishrag, I fell across his back, rampant and aching from desire. My groin fit against his butt. It took a minute for him to recover. In the meantime, I humped his trim ass.

"Wha'...you doin'? Man, stop that. We'll fight some more, but you ain't gonna do that to me."

"I just want to see one thing," I said, getting to my knees and pulling him to all fours hard against my groin. I fumbled with his belt.

"What you doing?" But he didn't shove me away. His resolve was weakening. I was wet inside my clothing.

"I asked you a question back at the club. Are you cut?"

"Yeah, I'm cut, man. Now leave me alone."

"I want to see for myself," I said calmly.

"Arright, but just to look."

I slipped his trousers and jockeys down to his knees and fingered his cock. He hadn't lied; he was circumcised. When it started to grow in my hand, he tried to pull up his trousers. I ground my hips against his naked butt and stroked his cock. It was bigger than I expected, given his lanky frame. Thick, but not overly long. The exposed head was bulbous. I cupped his balls.

"Man, come on!"

I reached back and stroked his crack, setting him to struggling again, but my knees were on his trousers, pinning his legs. Calmly, I undid my own pants and pulled him back to me. My cock rode against his buns. He moaned as I pushed him flat on his stomach. He didn't say a word.

"I won't do anything you don't want me to do, Lonnie. Just tell me no, and I'll let you up."

He moaned and shivered, but didn't say no. I ran the tip of my wet cock up and down his butt. Then I parted his buns with my hands and stroked his rosebud with my dripping tool. He froze like a deer caught in the headlights. His sphincter parted, and my glans slipped inside him.

"Ow!" he yelled and tried to rise, driving my cock deep into his channel.

I lay atop him, running my hands up his long back, playing over the knobs of his spine and across his broad shoulders, fighting to keep from assaulting him savagely. I lost the battle and began to hunch against his hard buns. He grunted. I pulled almost all the way out and slowly drove my shaft as deep as it would go. He mumbled something. I did it again. And again. Harder. Faster.

I tried to keep from coming too quickly, but it had been a long time. My breath came faster; I was getting there. My belly against his buttocks, my balls slapping his legs, my penis stroking his channel...it was getting to me.

Suddenly, I pulled his butt into the air and stood on my knees, ramming it to him harder and harder. I reached around and grasped his cock...turgid and ready to explode. He growled deep in his throat as I stroked him in time to my thrusts. Damn, he was hard.

Suddenly, I came with a deep groan. He let out a yelp, and his butt clamped down on my cock as his warm seed spilled out over my hand while mine spurted deep into his intestines. We both groaned again. He fell to his belly; I rode him down, and we lay there for a few moments while we recovered.

I rose and cleaned us with a canteen of water from my car. Lonnie watched me silently as I washed him after I got myself presentable.

"I want to see you again," I said as he got up and pulled his clothing into place.

He refused to look at me. I barely heard his answer. "Yeah."

I told him where I'd be at ten the following Friday night and watched his pickup out of sight. I would see him once more, but after that the magic would be gone. He probably wouldn't turn gay, but I was willing to bet he'd find himself a kid his own age for a little on the side now and then.

Actually, I saw Lonnie twice more, a tribute to his machismo. Even after a butt fucking, the kid hung on to his masculinity, but when it appeared that he was getting to like the arrangement too much, I cut it off.

I got off on macho guys, straight men with a little bit of defensiveness, a chink in the he-man image. Sensitivity, I'd always called it, but it was probably someone sending subtle signals he might be receptive to experimenting. I went for guys who'd battle for their manhood to the point where they could rationalize they'd fought the good fight before taking a cock up the ass.

I sighed aloud. There was no sign of that defensiveness in Airman John Deer. That was the reason I hadn't faced him down. The knowledge brought neither acceptance nor relief. The mere sight of the hunky airman in the hallway set me to aching. I prowled the nightclubs after duty hours and found a few potential targets, but they didn't stir me to action.

Another month passed, during which time Deer got a promotion and new assignment to a data-inputting position. I was pleased for him, although I saw less of him. Once again, he upset my apple cart.

"Sergeant Ryer," he called one noon as we passed in the hall. "You haven't been on the basketball court lately. Afraid of the competition?"

God! I'd never wanted anyone more in my life. "Hello, Deer. Been a little busy. But I like competition. Maybe if I had a little more, I'd come out again."

He laughed. "I believe that was a personal challenge, and I accept."

I motioned out the double doors toward the court beyond the smoking area. Nothing stirred except autumn leaves in a stiff breeze. "It's cold and windy out there."

"Excuses, excuses," John sang in his erotic baritone.

"All right, you're on. One on one."

Five minutes later, John went into a crouch, dribbled the ball in-bounds and double faked me to drop the ball cleanly through the net. That pissed me off, and for the next thirty minutes it was frenzied activity punctuated by grunts, growls and occasional shouts of triumph. Eventually, he netted two goals straight and howled with glee.

"Good game." I wiped sweat from my face as I followed Deer's tall frame back to the enlisted men's locker room where we stripped side by side. I hit the showers first; John took the one right across from me. Except for us, the place was deserted. We scrubbed in silence until he paused and looked over at me.

"Something wrong, Sarge?"

I reacted to his attention and quickly turned away. "No, why?"

"I don't know. You're acting sorta funny." There was a tremor in his voice that gave me a full erection. "Did I do something?"

Suddenly tired of the game, I lost my cool and turned to face him. "Yeah, you do something to me."

The shock on his face when he saw my throbbing cock should have struck me mute. It didn't. "I've been avoiding you to keep my fucking hands off you. Cripes, you don't make it easy."

He stared for a long moment before turning off the water and stalking stiff-legged into the locker area, snagging a towel along the way. Ashamed, I remained in the shower a minute longer, allowing my condition to cool. He was gone by the time I came into the changing area. That was the reaction I hated the most. It was final and unsatisfactory, bringing no physical release of any sort. On the other hand, I had no desire to beat up on Airman John Deer.

I didn't get much work done the rest of the afternoon, and stopped off at a bar on East Central for a stiff drink after retreat. I almost made a move on a muscled dude but recognized it was just a crude effort to get into a fight. At home, I changed, ate out of the refrigerator and finally had enough of TV pablum. I switched off the set, grabbed my keys and went outside. Screw it! I'd go find somebody to fuck or fight.

As I approached my car, a slight motion spun me around. John stood ten feet away, glaring at me. I didn't wait for him to speak.

"I'm sorry, John. I should have kept my feelings to myself. I apologize."

"Why, Master Sergeant?" he asked formally.

"Stupidity on my part."

"That's not what I meant. Why do you feel that way about me?"

"Cripes, John! Take a good look in the mirror. You're a good-looking fucker."

Even in the darkness I could see his head shake. His hair grabbed the streetlight and flashed like a beacon. "You're a man. I'm a man. Why'd you come on to me?"

"That should be obvious. I'm gay, John. I like guys."

His shrug was almost imperceptible. "Then go find another queer."

I leaned against the side of my car. "It doesn't work like that for me. I like straight guys. Or guys who think they're straight."

"What the fuck does that mean?"

I sighed. "Sometimes I see a little uncertainty in a guy, a clue or hint he won't go ballistic if I come on to him. Oh, he'll put up a fuss, but deep down he won't mean it."

He took a step or two closer. "That's what you think you saw me in?"

"Frankly, no. I let myself get out of control."

"*Did* you see that in me? Tell me the truth."

"No, I didn't. But I was hoping to see it and…well, I fell in love with you."

He took a step backward. "I don't swing that way, man. You keep your distance; I'll keep mine. And that'll be the end of it. I won't get you thrown out of the Air Force."

"Agreed." I wanted to offer a hand but knew he'd misunderstand.

I stood there for five minutes after he left before returning to the house, all desire to go nightclubbing evaporated. Instead, I sat before the blank TV screen, picturing John naked in the shower, shock on his face as he saw my hard-on. The water had been running down all the crevices of his body I wanted to explore.

I gradually relaxed as the week passed and it became clear Deer had held his tongue, as promised. Although I had to come to grips with losing a friendship that had been valuable to me. Following a security management meeting on Friday afternoon, I dragged my tired butt home after retreat. The tension of the past few days had taken its toll. I had to force myself to eat and clean up. Dressed in old cutoff sweats, I found a book and spent an hour reading the same three or four pages before the door-bell rang. Irritated and out of sorts, I threw open the door and froze. A thoroughly soused John Deer swayed on my doorstep.

"Fuck you, Master Sergeant," he growled by way of greeting.

"You're drunk, John." It was all I could do to keep from touching him.

"Not's drunk as I'm gonna be." He lurched inside and fell into a chair. "Gimme a drink."

"Nothing in the house," I lied. He sure as shit didn't need more booze.

"Knew you wouldn't give me nothing anyway." He lumbered to his feet and seized the front of my shirt. "Oughta beat the shit outa you, you queer asshole. Disrespecting another airman like that."

"I guess I owe you something, John," I said slowly, "but I'm not sure it's a beating. I'll sober you up. Give you a place to sleep it off. But that's all."

"You'll take whatever I wanta give you." His scowl was ugly

now. He jerked hard on my shirt. The thing was almost as old as I was, and the seams gave way. Suddenly, I was shirtless. He glared at my bare torso through blurry eyes. "Thought all you white motherfuckers were hairy."

"Not me. So I guess I'm not a mother—" I bit off my words as he ripped my cutoffs away, leaving me standing in the wreckage of my clothing.

John's eyes raked my nakedness. "Queer bastard," he mumbled. For a moment I thought he was passing out, but he roused himself. "Take off my shirt, you fairy, faggot son-of-a-bitch." His voice cracked a little.

His naked chest glowed from sweat and alcohol as I lifted his shirt over his head. Without his asking, I reached for his belt buckle, pausing a moment before sliding his trousers down the well-shaped thighs.

"Get on your fucking knees."

The sight of his beautiful cock, the flat, hairless belly, the heavy balls quelled the anger rising in me. Obediently, I dropped before him, steadying myself with a hand on his hard, brown thighs.

"Take it, asshole!" It failed as a snarl, sounding more like a plea.

Gingerly, I leaned forward to touch his navel with my lips. He shuddered as I slid down into the curly pubic hair, rubbing my chin in the soft mass. His cock pressed against my neck. He smelled of alcohol and manliness and desire. I lowered my head, riding over his fat glans and sucking him into my mouth. It had been a long time, but it felt good and natural. Instantly, he was hard; his massive bulk filled my mouth as it lengthened.

"Suck it," he gasped, a trace of desperation in his voice. "Take it." His hands cupped the back of my head. He pulled me forward and lunged against me. Understanding his desperate need, I accommodated as much of him as possible. The part I could not swallow, I grasped with one hand as he fucked my face, hunching his way toward orgasm. I played with his balls and stroked his ass. He began to grunt and coo and groan, thrusting harder and harder. Then he came, blowing his balls in a sudden gush of cum. Desperately he ground himself against me a couple of more times before I took over, riding up and down his towering cock, sucking all the cum his balls could deliver.

When he pushed me away, John took a shaky breath or two and abruptly sat down hard on the couch behind him. Within seconds he was out. I arranged him on the sofa, stripping away his boots and the clothing bunched around his feet. As excited as I have ever been, I stood over his unconscious form and jerked myself to climax, spasming all over his inert body. I collapsed atop him, my cheek alongside his. With my cum drying between us, I kissed his lips and his eyes until my excitement died away. Afterward, I cleaned him up, drew a light blanket over him and retired to my bed to relive the night.

I knew the moment he came in the room, but feigned sleep, watching him in the darkness through half-closed lids. He drew the sheet back and stood studying me.

"I'm not through with you yet, motherfucker," he muttered before falling upon me.

And he wasn't. I've fucked guys so long and hard that they've begged for mercy. That's what John did to me. He almost brought a protest when he reached for me the third time sometime after dawn, but he turned me on my back and mounted me from the front so I could watch his performance. My cry of "uncle" died on my lips as I saw again what he was preparing to shove into me. It was long and thick and absolutely straight like some dangerous, gleaming, primitive stone lance. He rode me like a stallion until I came without touching my cock. As I was spurting, he bucked wildly and shot into me, shouting curses and muttering dark deprecations that sounded to my ears like tender endearments.

TAXICAB
CONFESSION

Gregory L. Norris

A brutal wind tore across the front yard. Ice rattled in the bare maples and rangy cedars along the driveway and sidewalk that demarcated 11 Park Street from its nearest neighbors. Caleb felt the chill through his trench coat and heard the tabernacle of wind against ice through the black knit cap pulled down over his ears. A bitch of a freeze had blown down from Canada, the coldest yet of the young winter. The furnace in the apartment had kicked on that afternoon while the sun was still out. He couldn't remember it switching off after that. The heat would probably run all night.

Caleb shifted his weight from one foot to the other. His toes felt the cold, too, despite thick boot socks. He checked his cell phone. No messages though his taxi was two minutes late, according to the tiny clock. Not really, he thought. Late didn't happen until five had gone by.

He exhaled a sigh. The breeze swept the locomotive breath past him and toward the hill, below which the city spread, the numerous golden lights from so many windows and the neon glow from businesses still open all sitting beneath a sky filled with pale stars. Caleb was about to turn back toward the apartment, abandoning the night's ridiculous mission, when the taxi pulled up to the curb. It was gray with navy details instead of yellow, like the cabs he was used to hailing in most big cities where work now took him. Caleb got in.

Warmth embraced him in the backseat. The smell of accumulated sweat, a trace of cologne, and the grime left behind by snowy boots that had ground salt into the carpet teased his nose.

"Hey," Caleb said.

The driver answered, "'Sup," and checked his clipboard before glancing into the rearview.

Caleb stole a look at the young man's face, reflected in the mirror. Wounded puppy-dog eyes, a warm chocolate brown, dark hair in an athlete's cut but with a bit of spike on the top and a strong jaw coated in a few hours' worth of five o'clock shadow drove the last of the chill from his bones.

"Lewis Lane, up in Ashland?"

"Yes," Caleb answered.

"That's a hike. Gonna cost you," the driver said.

"It'll cost me more if I don't. I can afford it."

The taxi driver flashed the barest smile, one corner of his mouth pulling into a meager grin. Not insignificant was the dimple that appeared. Caleb's gaze lingered. Mid-twenties, he guessed, and supremely attractive, maybe one of the handsomest dudes he'd crossed paths with, since—

"It's your lucky night," the driver said.

Caleb choked down a dry swallow and looked away. "Yeah, how's that?"

"So many cars broken down with dead batteries, we're stretched to the max. I agreed to stay until things catch up."

"Lucky me."

"If this was tomorrow night, I wouldn't be here. Not with the hockey game on."

Caleb's eyes wandered back to the rearview. In the glare of the streetlamp and dashboard lights, he saw that the driver wore a black sweatshirt displaying the trademark of Boston's pro hockey team.

"Bruins fan, huh?"

"Fuck yeah, man. The game tomorrow night's gonna be a real ball buster. Can't wait for it."

"Thanks for the heads-up. I'll be sure to watch it."

The taxi whisked down Park, turned right on Newcombe, and was on Winter Street before the driver asked, "What's up in Ashland?"

Caleb hesitated. "Nothing too important."

"Has to be for you to haul your ass that kind of distance on the coldest fuckin' night of the year."

Caleb shrugged while studying the young man's neck, hairline and ears. Drawing in a deep breath, he imagined how great the driver's body would smell up close after a full shift behind the wheel. Jimmy's always had after an honest day's work. So would this dude's. "What's your name?"

The driver said, "Deke."

Caleb smiled in response. He liked it. An honest, blue-collar hockey fan's sort of name. "Nice to meet you, Deke."

Deke tipped him the chin in the mirror, that universal gesture of respect between males that makes instant buddies out of men who've only just met. Not that they'd be complete strangers by the end of this trip, Caleb sensed; Ashland was six or seven towns north of Haven Hill. That kind of distance was due to force some kind of conversation, perhaps confession, even between men of few words.

Wind rocked the taxi. They came to a set of lights. A dusty curtain of powder—rock salt or icy snow leftover from the previous day's storm, likely a dry stew of both—spirited past. The traffic lights swung in the wind.

"Cold fuckin' night to be out," Deke said.

Caleb nodded. "At least it's not because of a dead battery."

They turned toward the highway. The on-ramp rose ahead of the taxi through another gray gust. "Mind me asking why we're headed all the way to Ashland?"

Caleb caught the young man's eyes in the rearview. The truth trembled on his lips. He gulped down the words, replacing them with ones that weren't so much a lie as a fib.

"Visiting an old friend," he said. "I used to live around here, long time ago. That place on Park Street I'm staying at, I lived there, too, for a while. It's my brother's. When I fly back after the holidays to catch up, I crash in his spare room. I make this trip back east once a year and try to stay warm."

"Good luck with that," Deke said.

Caleb eyed him the best he could from his position in the backseat. How much he looked like Jimmy had in those long-past years shocked him. "What about you?"

"What about me," Deke grumbled, phrasing his response as a statement instead of a question.

"You originally from around here?"

"Yeah, but not for much longer. I'm getting out. Gonna go up north, join a hockey league and play in my free time. That's what I want to do. I'm gonna."

"Good for you," Caleb said. At that moment, he was more like Jimmy than Caleb had imagined possible—impulsive, passionate.

"Yup, play hockey, maybe drive a truck or a taxi if they have a service in town, and chill."

"The north country makes Ashland look like a cakewalk."

Deke pushed the taxi up to seventy on the highway's posted sixty-five. "It's your dollar, dude."

They didn't say much for the next fifteen miles. Deke pulled off Exit 51-B, traveled along Main, over a bridge, and down a hill, making a left after the post office, onto Lewis Lane.

"Which place you want again?" he asked.

Caleb's pulse raced. "Number Seventeen, up there on the left. The gray one."

Only it wasn't gray anymore, and it hadn't been in a decade.

"Looks yellow to me."

"It's always gray in my memories," Caleb said.

The ranch house sat wreathed in hedges of juniper and strings of white Christmas lights, which lent the place an aura. Two SUVs sat parked in the driveway. Jimmy used to drive a jeep. The ghostly telltale of the TV flickered in the living room.

"Pull over there," Caleb said, indicating the side of the road, where naked willow trees stood guard beside a frozen brook. No hockey had ever been played on the small fire pond connected to the brook, but Caleb conjured visions of other sweaty times spent beneath those trees.

"Now what?" Deke asked.

"Just give me a minute or two," Caleb said.

A heavy silence settled over the taxi. Caleb settled back and gazed out the window, seeing a yellow house but also a gray one; the winter but also the summer. It was someone else's home now, but also one where he'd lived, with Jimmy.

Reaching his hand down, Caleb fumbled between the trench's buttons. His dick was hard. It probably had been since hopping into Deke's taxi, his maleness gorged and excited just from being in the other man's presence. Another few seconds, and he'd seen enough. "Okay, we can go now."

Deke turned around. Caleb's hand flew off his crotch.

"Huh?" the driver asked. "Dude, we just got here."

"I know."

A cocky grin broke on the corner of Deke's mouth, but didn't grow much bigger, only enough to restore that incredible dimple. Maybe that was what had given him wood, thought Caleb. Deke the driver's little dimple-conjuring magic trick.

"She must have been fuckin' hot, dude."

Not sure why, Caleb confessed. "*He* was."

The silence returned. For a short, damning sum of seconds that felt more like minutes, Caleb worried that he was being judged. The driver's smile flattened; his dimple vanished. Dark eyes, chocolate brown, darted away when they met in the mirror.

"Sure you're ready to head back?" Deke eventually asked.

"Yeah, I'm sure."

Deke put the car in drive. Turned onto the road. Accelerated.

"So, this dude, what was he like?

"His name was Jimmy," said Caleb, "and he looked a lot like you."

Caleb confessed the rest: How, like a lot of guys on September 12, 2001, Jimmy had dropped everything, signed up and was shipped overseas; how James Joseph Duncan had taken a fatal bullet in a remote place colder than this shitty night, on the other side of the world; how Caleb, unable to stand it, had moved to the West Coast after the tragedy just to feel warm again.

"That fuckin sucks, all of it," Deke said.

"It is what it is."

Then, just shy of the highway, Deke said, "Tell me more about this hot dude that I remind you of."

"He had the best dick, and I loved sucking on it," Caleb said frankly, just like that.

Deke studied him in the rearview. This time, he didn't glance away when their eyes met.

Caleb piled into the front seat. His heart raced as lights dimmed. Deke had parked in the apartment building's lot, in the corner farthest away from the streetlamp. They were alone now, effectively in the dark. The taxi idled.

"You're sure about this?" Caleb asked.

Deke grunted and showed him that he was by grabbing the back of Caleb's head and guiding him down between Deke's legs. The position pinned his face between hockey sweatshirt and steering wheel. There, he caught a whiff of the young man's scent, the clean smell of a man's skin and a hint of male musk. Caleb reached toward Deke's crotch. The front of the driver's jeans was already tented in anticipation. Stiff flesh pulsed beneath his fingertips. Deke grunted. While fumbling open zipper and unbuckling belt, Caleb relived the leg of their return journey that had led to this moment.

You suck dick? Bet you're great at it.

Ever had yours—?

Naw, into chicks, but you got me curious now. Your friend, he liked it?

No complaints, only...

What?

Caleb had gulped, telegraphing in actions instead of words.

You swallow? Fuck, dude...you want to suck me?

Huh?

Deke's fingers pushed again, transporting Caleb back to the future. "Suck me," he commanded.

Caleb pulled at Deke's underwear—black boxer-briefs, by

the look of them in the wan glow filtering in from outside and the dashboard's lights. Lifting Deke's sweatshirt and the black T-shirt beneath, his eyes followed the line of coarse fur that cut Deke down the center, making a ring around his belly button, before joining a thick pelt of crotch hair.

Caleb pulled harder. An upwardly curved cock sprang forth, thickened at the thrill of meeting Caleb's warm mouth on this coldest of nights. With it, the most magnificent of male smells tempted Caleb's nose: dense fur, balls and the heat of a man's most powerful flesh. Tucking the elastic waistband under Deke's meaty nuts unleashed a feeling of déjà vu. He'd done this same thing to Jimmy more than once behind the wheel of his jeep. Only Jimmy was gone. This was Deke, a stranger. A very handsome one.

"Yeah, pull on my sac, dude," the stranger huffed.

Caleb did. Lips parted, he walked his mouth over Deke's straining dickhead. Inching lower, he tasted salt.

Got a girlfriend?

No one special, and the last one didn't like sucking my dick.

Shame. You're really attractive.

And my balls are really blue, dude. We get back, how about you come up front, hum on my bone. I'll consider it my tip...

Crisp curls tickled Caleb's nostrils. His chin scraped Deke's nuts. The thickness between his lips pulsed, so warm, so immediate. Deke wasn't Jimmy, but the taxi driver had made him feel fully alive for the first time in way too long. He lifted his mouth up, his memory recording length, girth, veins, hair, scent. Opening wider, he plunged back down.

Deke exhaled a breathy, *"Fuck!"*

Caleb didn't need to ask if he was doing a good job; he knew it by Deke's grin when he gazed up and saw the man's dimple was out, inspired by a wide, happy grin. Caleb mentally called up the playbook of trustworthy tricks and trotted out a few: moaning around Deke's dick, caressing it not only with lips, gums, and tongue but the vibrations of his vocal cords; gently tickling the underside of his shaft with tongue curls; grasping the dude's balls with varying degrees of pressure.

After a few minutes of hard sucking, Caleb regurgitated Deke's cock and licked it like a lollipop, up and down the shaft, around the underside of the head, finally attending to the piss-hole, which was gummed up with salty tears. The entire time, Caleb held it by forefinger and thumb clamped in a chokehold around its hairy root.

He slapped it against his cheek, hard enough to send strings of precome across his face. And then he went back down, sucking Deke to the balls.

"Oh, fuck, dude," Deke sighed. "Keep doing that, yeah, swallow my fuckin' bone!"

Up and down, working the dude's balls. Not long after, Deke tensed and emptied his balls into Caleb's mouth.

A damp fog had formed on the inside of the windshield. Caleb swallowed and lifted up, seeing the fresh perspiration on the windows as well as Deke's face, smelling it on his next breath.

"Let me clean you up," Caleb said.

He lowered back down and lapped the dregs off Deke's dripping cock, stealing a few more licks across his balls in the deal. Another suck, and then Deke nudged him away.

"Keep it up and I'm gonna want some more."

"Good. I'm ready."

"But I have to fly, dude, seriously."

Caleb pulled out his wallet and paid his fare. "Thanks, man."

Deke adjusted his junk, tucked everything back in and zipped. "Yeah, and you got a little something extra for your money."

Caleb reached for the door handle. His own dick ached, and he planned to attend to its needs after having taken care of Deke's. "You tasted great. You have an amazing cock. Second best I've ever known."

He opened the door. The light came on. A gust of air, miserably cold, charged into the taxi.

"Dude," the taxi driver said, calling him back.

Caleb leaned down through the door, and there was handsome Deke, a business card extended in hand.

"You need a ride anywhere, ask for me. You want another load out of my big old balls, the number to my cell's on the back. Don't call me tomorrow, though—unless you want to watch the hockey game with me and, you know..."

Caleb licked his lips again, pocketed the card and turned toward the apartment building's entrance, warmed inside against the brutal cold.

PISTOL WHIPPED

D. Fostalove

He was the type of guy women hated. They hated him because he was a man, through and through, not one of those lisping, limp-wristed queens they laughed at on television. They hated him because they couldn't spot him a mile away and befriend him before he scooted up next to their boyfriends or husbands. They hated him because he could do things to their husbands they couldn't do.

He knew all of this. He could see it in their icy stares as their men's heads turned ever so slightly in his direction when he walked by them. He didn't mind their disdain for him and men like him. His only concern was getting his rocks off with whomever he chose, married, single or somewhere in between. His sexual appetite and thirst for the touch of a man was all that mattered while out on the prowl. This time, like many others, was no different.

He walked into one of his frequent pickup spots, a small diner in downtown Charlotte, and sat at a booth behind one where a couple was seated, engaged in a lively conversation about a cruise they'd recently been on. He could tell from the quick glance out the corner of the ruggedly attractive man's eye that he was *down*. His girlfriend probably hadn't noticed the slight exchange between them as she chattered on about the sea turtles and stingrays she'd swam among during their trip.

Not ten minutes had passed before the girlfriend sauntered across the diner to the ladies' room and he heard the raspy voice whisper over his shoulder.

"What's your name?"

"Grayson." That was what he always told them. He'd acquired the nickname from his father, who would always refer to him as his "gray-eyed son."

"You down?"

"It's whatever." The waitress returned with the slice of raspberry cheesecake he'd ordered. Grayson never came to the mom-and-pop diner to eat. He would always order something light and usually end up with his purchase in a doggy bag for his girlfriend, depending on how quickly he found a suitable conquest.

"You gay?" The man asked in a rushed whisper as the waitress moved on to assist another customer.

"Nah." For all intents and purposes, Grayson was straight. He had a girlfriend and a three-year-old son. They lived together in an apartment on the north side of the city. He loved and took care of them before he thought of his own needs and wants. "You?"

"No," the man spat.

Grayson didn't care much for labels. It was the men who crossed his path, some of them, who felt the need to explain themselves, as if he was judging them. He was no judge, jury or executioner, although he'd been with them all: congressmen, scientists, drug dealers, judges, corrections officers, preachers, truckers, professional athletes and college professors.

He understood that men like the one seated behind him evaded men who identified as gay like Europeans once tried to avoid the bubonic plague. Gay men were more effeminate, flamboyant and judgmental. At least that's what Grayson had been told. He never dealt with them; he and they didn't live the same lives, frequent the same spots or have anything in common outside of sex.

"What are you getting into after you leave here?"

"You, if you're lucky." Grayson looked up as the man's girlfriend returned, smiling politely as she walked by. He smiled back and looked across the diner, catching the eye of a muscular man with skin the color of a coconut who was seated at a table near the window sipping a cup of coffee. Seeing this man, Grayson was no longer interested in the man behind him and focused all of his attention on the new guy. Not in all of his years of meeting and freaking dudes on the low had Grayson felt so compelled to approach a man as he was at that moment.

He would make eye contact and exchange a simple greeting, but they would always have to initiate the first move before he sealed the deal. This time, it was different. Without a second thought, Grayson walked across the bustling diner and took a seat across from the man who slowly glanced up from the newspaper set next to a fresh plate of sunny-side-up eggs, sausage links, cheese grits and toast.

"What's up?" the man said coolly.

"What are you reading?" Grayson asked, averting his eyes to the paper.

The man pressed a thick index finger into the middle of the page. "Article on Prop Eight."

"Not sure what that is but okay." Grayson stole a glance at

him and instantly thought of how the man favored a younger Ving Rhames in build and facial features, minus the mustache.

The man smiled but didn't look up from the paper. "I didn't think you would."

He reeked of danger. The forcefulness with which he spoke, the way his eyes bore into Grayson as he shifted his gaze between the paper and the plate of food caused Grayson's heart to pound with excitement. He wanted to know who this man was, where he'd come from and what he did more than what he occupied his time with reading. Was he in town on business or pleasure? Maybe a combination?

"You didn't come to see what I was reading," the man said with a mouth full of food.

"Nah, I didn't."

"State your business." He wiped the sides of his mouth with a napkin and waited.

Grayson leaned in and lowered his voice. "I noticed you across the room. I wanted to see what's up with you."

The man nodded toward the booth Grayson had been sitting in earlier. "What's up with your boy over there who keeps glaring in this direction? He got a problem?"

"He's nobody," Grayson said, forgetting about the man as soon as the words left his lips.

After shoveling another forkful of food into his mouth, the man said, "Name's Tank."

Grayson provided his name. Tank extended his hand across the table. Grayson shook it, feeling the strength in it. He doubted the man's name was really Tank but found it suitable, like his. Tank was built like the armored combat vehicle. With each movement, muscles rippled and flexed over his body. Even the muscles in his neck bulged as he chewed his food. Watching Tank eat and read the newspaper, Grayson thought of what a powerful lover he probably was, tossing his eager partners from position to position with ease.

"When I'm through, we can head out. I'm at that Omni a few blocks away from the Bobcats Arena on Trade Street."

After eating, Tank tossed a twenty-dollar bill on the table, grabbed the newspaper and got up. The waitress returned with Grayson's carryout container and receipt for the cheese-cake. Grayson paid in cash and followed Tank out, the rejected conquest fidgeting uncomfortably as they walked by him.

"You want to follow me in your ride?"

"I caught the CATS bus downtown," Grayson lied. He didn't want to risk having Tank slip from his grasp just as he had slithered away from the disgruntled reject at the diner. It wasn't that Grayson thought Tank would ditch him, from the way they sized each other up before heading out, but he wanted to make sure this one didn't get away. There was something about Tank that piqued his sexual curiosity unlike any other man he'd encountered in recent memory.

In the short ride to Tank's hotel, they talked and Grayson actually listened. Tank was a bodyguard for a starlet wildly popular with the Disney crowd. Prior to working as a body-guard, he'd been a bounty hunter for nearly ten years. He'd shot several fugitives and killed "a handful of them motherfuckers." He'd been shot on three separate occasions and stabbed in the chest once. He had fraternal twins, a girl and a boy. He was divorced from their mother but fucked her occasionally and her sister when he wasn't away on business and messing around with men on the side.

After entering Tank's hotel room separately, Grayson continued their conversation from the car but realized Tank was no longer interested in talking. Tank placed a leather case he'd pulled from the glove box of his SUV onto the nightstand

and sat on the edge of the bed. He patted a spot next to him. Grayson, taking in the view of the city from the tenth-story window, walked across the room and took a seat next to Tank, who immediately reached for the buttons on Grayson's shirt.

"I don't have a lot of time," Tank said. "Tatiana is a guest speaker at a sickle-cell fundraiser tonight and has to be on a flight back to New York by midnight to shoot her television show in the morning."

Grayson tried to keep his mouth from dropping open at Tank's admission that he was the bodyguard of one of the top-grossing young stars in the United States. It couldn't be the same girl. "Are you talking about the girl who's the voice of the wisecracking turtle on that Saturday morning animated series, the one with her own sitcom on the cartoon channel? Tatiana Parish?"

"Yeah, that's her," Tank said, more focused on removing Grayson's shirt than his conversation.

"My son loves that stupid, smart-mouthed turtle."

Tank tapped his wrist where a watch would've been and repeated that he didn't have that much time before he was scheduled to escort the young actress from her suite at the end of the hall to the fundraiser before they made their trek back to NYC. Grayson glanced at his watch, thinking they had at least two hours before the sun set. That would be plenty of time for him to get a nut and be on his way before his girlfriend returned from her shift as assistant manager at the local phone company's call center. He leaned back on his hands as Tank undid the last button of his shirt and pulled it away, revealing a toned, lightly haired chest.

Grazing Grayson's chest with a massive paw, Tank engulfed one of the younger, slimmer man's nipples while yanking at Grayson's belt buckle. Tank fondled Grayson's other nipple while still sucking on the one in his mouth. He unzipped Grayson's jeans and reached inside for the engorged flesh throbbing beneath a pair of cotton boxer-briefs. When he found it, Tank stopped sucking the nipple and yanked at Grayson's jeans and boxers until they were jumbled at his knees.

Tank then opened his mouth wide and engulfed the erect appendage, slowly sliding it in and out of his mouth, savoring the sweat-salty taste. Grayson closed his eyes, enjoying the suction as Tank bobbed back and forth, circling his dickhead with his tongue. Palming the back of Tank's head, Grayson controlled the pace of the bodyguard's movements. He tilted his head toward the ceiling and moaned out, somewhat shocked at how skilled Tank was at giving head. He wanted to return the favor.

Grayson grabbed Tank's shoulders and gently forced him away from his dick. "Get up. I want to eat that big ass up."

Tank, still on his knees eyeballing Grayson's saliva-soaked dick while stroking his own piece through his zipper, shook his head. "I have something else in mind."

Before Grayson could say anything, Tank stripped down, leaving his clothing in a pile at his feet. He walked over to the nightstand and retrieved the leather case. Grayson watched curiously as Tank tossed the case into his lap and climbed onto the bed. Grayson looked at it resting on his thighs, wondering what Tank expected him to do with the Bible he assumed was inside. The only thing he'd prayed for was that Tank's sex was as thrilling as his sculpted, tattoo-riddled body. So far, he was impressed.

"Open it."

Grayson touched the case but didn't move to unzip it. "What is it?"

Tank insisted he open it. When Grayson looked down at it

but didn't make any further movements to open it, Tank sat up from his reclining position and snatched it from Grayson's lap. He unzipped the case and retrieved a gun from inside. Tank pointed it in Grayson's direction, saying nothing. Grayson glared at the stainless steel 9mm with a wood grip, his heart thumping wildly in his chest. The glistening weapon was alluring, like the idea of inserting a car key into an electrical outlet was to toddlers, but he understood its danger, especially when pointed at his vital organs.

He'd been in hundreds of different scenarios with men, from back alleys with dope boys to fire escapes with cheating husbands to curtained-off ICUs with cardiologists, but never had he been presented with a man pointing a gun at his chest. If he'd known there was a possibility the bodyguard had intentions of robbing or killing him, he would have stuck with the man in the diner. Grayson thought about his son and his girlfriend hearing he'd been murdered in an upscale hotel downtown when he should've been at work and running errands on his lunch break.

Just as Grayson was going to retrieve his wallet and warn Tank that there was only a maxed-out credit card and about ten dollars inside, Tank twirled the gun around in his hand so the barrel was pointed in his direction. Tank looked at the gun in his extended hand and then lowered his gaze to Grayson's hands that were clasped in his lap.

"Take it," he said.

Grayson was so preoccupied with visions of his girlfriend and child crying that he hadn't heard Tank clearly. "What?"

Tank scooted forward on the bed and grabbed one of Grayson's hands. He smacked the gun into Grayson's open palm and made him form a fist around the handle. Grayson looked at the cold steel in his hand before he glanced at Tank, who maneuvered to the middle of the bed on all fours.

"Can you feel the power in it?" Tank asked as he remained on all fours in the middle of the bed.

Grayson did feel its power. He'd held guns before and even pointed one at an old running buddy he caught fucking his ex-girlfriend, but never had he pulled the trigger and never had he held one that he was sure had been used to kill someone. He had no idea why Tank had pulled the gun out in the middle of their sexing or why he was being forced to hold it, but he wanted to toss it over his shoulder, pull his pants up and make a mad dash toward the door.

"Does it have your heart beating fast?"

"Yes," Grayson admitted.

"Gets your adrenaline pumping, doesn't it?"

Grayson nodded.

"Mine too," Tank said, his tone oozing with raw sexuality. "Give it to me."

Grayson was more than willing to return the weapon but when he attempted to hand it back to Tank, the bodyguard shook his head and looked over his shoulder toward his ass. Realizing what Tank had unveiled the gun for, his eyes widened. A smirk appeared on Tank's face at Grayson's sudden realization. Tank reached into the case and retrieved a bottle of lube before he rolled it across the bed in Grayson's direction.

Reaching for the lubricant, Grayson flipped the lid and began rubbing the liquid over the barrel like it was a thick silver dick. "Is it loaded?"

"Fully." Tank watched in eager anticipation as Grayson removed his jeans, underwear and shirt and climbed into the bed. He moved behind Tank with the gun raised toward the ceiling and took a deep breath. "Put your finger on the trigger when you run that bitch in and out of me."

Grayson slowly brought the gun down to Tank's ass and pressed the muzzle between his muscular cheeks. Tank, gazing back fervently, backed himself onto the gun. With each of Tank's pushes against the gun, Grayson flinched, thinking it would go off and kill the bodyguard. Seeing Grayson's apprehension about the whole thing, Tank spoke with the same forcefulness he'd used when initially speaking with him and demanded he calm down.

"I've never done anything like this before," Grayson said.

"There's a first time for everything," Tank responded. "Now relax, man."

Grayson exhaled and steadied his shaking hand. He looked at Tank who nodded for him to proceed. Grayson carefully inserted the greasy weapon into Tank's waiting hole as the bodyguard groaned and wiggled to conform to the unyielding steel. When the trigger guard connected with Tank's flesh, Grayson stopped and waited for his next directive.

"Imagine that nine is your dick," Tank said. "Show me what you'd do to my hole."

Grayson remembered then that his goal was getting *his* rocks off and not submitting to the sexual demands of anyone other than his girlfriend. He told Tank to lie on his side and when he did, Grayson positioned himself on the bed so his feet were at Tank's head and vice versa. Without saying a word, Tank scooted up and slurped Tank's flaccid dick into his mouth. Grayson lifted one of Tank's mammoth thighs and cautiously slid the barrel back into his ass. Tank moaned out as the cold steel entered him and coaxed Grayson to go faster, harder and deeper.

Obliging, Grayson increased the frequency with which the gun entered and exited Tank. Tank's dick-sucking matched the speed of Grayson's gun thrusts. The strong sensations

Tank created in his groin with his advanced oral skills eased Grayson's nerves. A single digit grazed the trigger. He fingered it with mounting excitement and a slight fear of the ensuing consequences if he were to press the trigger and fire a shot into Tank's sweaty, gyrating body. He closed his eyes and thought of the power in his hands, the muscular man groaning loudly as Grayson thrust the steel weapon into his guts. He felt himself nearing climax from the thoroughness of Tank's lips and tongue devouring his dick while he cupped his balls in a large hand, rolling them over his palm like a pair of treasured dice.

Grayson didn't want to bust a nut from head alone, so he pulled away from Tank's powerful jaws and removed the gun from his ass. He crawled down the bed and forced Tank onto his stomach. Tank stuck his ass out and reached back to his sweaty, lube-covered hole and slid his middle finger inside. Grayson reached over the bed for his jeans, looking for the condoms he always carried with him.

"Nah. Fuck me raw with that big ass pipe."

He never fucked anyone raw but his girlfriend, no matter how tempting or persuasive a man was. Grayson retrieved a condom from his pocket against Tank's protests, tore the wrapper and rolled it over his pulsating dick. He squeezed between Tank's legs and plowed into him like a battering ram. Caught off guard by the suddenness of Grayson's entering, Tank winced and cried out in agony. He squirmed beneath Grayson and buried his head in the pillows as the man gripped his hips and pounded him unmercifully. Tank hadn't expected Grayson to be so rough, after his initial trepidation when presented with the gun, but the surprise of his brutishness excited him.

"Come on. Fuck the dog shit out of me."

Grayson palmed Tank's head and forced it into the mattress as he thrust all ten of his thick inches into him with no regard for the muffled cries or the hand Tank tried to use in a futile attempt to slow down the pace of Grayson's movements. Grayson fucked the bodyguard with an intensity matching the fear he'd felt when Tank pointed the gun at him. He wanted to shock Tank just as much as he had been when he realized the man's purpose for producing the gun. He wanted to show that getting penetrated by any inanimate object dulled in comparison to getting fucked by a skilled man with a big-ass dick and stamina similar to that of a decathlete.

"Tell me you like how this good dick stretches your insides."

Tank moaned an inaudible response.

"I can't hear you," Grayson said. "Do I have to fuck a response out of you?"

"Yes." Tank climbed up onto his hands and knees and threw his ass back.

Grayson clamped a hand on the back of Tank's neck and one hand around his waist and continued stuffing him with his inches. Tank grabbed his dick and began stroking it. Moments later, he exploded in ragged spurts onto the comforter below and growled a round of curses. Grayson suddenly pulled out, ripped the condom off and released himself, white globs shooting up the mountains and valleys of Tank's chiseled back.

Exhausted, Grayson wanted to collapse atop Tank and take a breather but knew a cuddle session wasn't appropriate or desired on either of their parts. He grabbed at the comforter and wiped his dick off before he stood and began dressing to leave. Tank crumpled onto the bed and rolled to his side, watching Grayson button his shirt and scan the room for his other garments.

"No round two?"

Grayson looked up from the floor where he was searching for one of his tennis shoes. "I have to pick my kid up from daycare and you have to go protect that celebrity girl."

"You're right." Tank reached for his semierect dick and began slowly stroking it again.

Finding his shoe, Grayson put it on and stood. He grabbed the brown bag with his cheesecake inside and looked at Tank, sprawled across the bed drenched in sweat. "I'll see you around."

Tank nodded. "You frequent that hole-in-the-wall diner much?"

"I stop through from time to time." Grayson reached for the door and glanced back, thinking about the trek to the diner where his car was parked. "Why?"

"If I'm ever in this city again, I'll stop through there. Maybe we'll cross paths again."

"Anything's possible."

TED AND BREAKFAST

Hank Edwards

The shadow of the east wing of the house lay halfway across the flagstone patio when I heard the tractor mower rev to life. I looked up from my book and watched the tractor amble across the verdant expanse, Ted sitting astride it with his shirt off.

I took in his broad, tanned chest and the layer of dark hair riding down his torso to spread over the flat of his belly. I tracked the hair as it ducked coyly beneath the sweat-stained waistband of the innkeeper's khaki shorts and I wondered if his balls were sweaty yet and how they would taste.

Ted caught me watching and raised a hand high in greeting, exposing the dark tuft of hair in his armpit as his teeth flashed white beneath his trim salt-and-pepper mustache. I waved back and waited until he had ridden the mower out of sight to adjust my hardening cock.

I was two days into a two-week vacation at this rambling bed and breakfast, the Blue Goose Inn, and I was starting to feel antsy. When I had booked the room a month ago, I was just getting over Vic, my longest relationship yet, and the solitude promised by the inn's website sounded like a soothing balm for my wounded ego. Now, however, I was starting to wonder if I'd made the right decision.

I had been told about the place by a coworker, and Ted had answered the phone when I called. When I told Ted the dates I had already scheduled for my vacation time, he explained with sincere apology that his wife was going to be out of town those two weeks and they had decided not to rent out any rooms during that time. This would give him the chance to do some maintenance work on the house and grounds without disturbing the guests. My disappointment must have been palpable in my disheartened response, because he took a breath and suddenly changed his tune, saying that one guest wouldn't keep him from his work, and booked my reservation.

The house was gorgeous, a flagstone manor built in the European style, with a grand history of rich owners who went bankrupt one after the other until the last owner sold it to Ted and his wife. There were eight bedrooms, each with its own bathroom and all tastefully decorated in various themes. My room took up the back corner of the house with windows that looked out over the rose gardens and the carriage house a few yards away where the owners lived. It was beautiful and surrounded by open country; a relaxing atmosphere designed to give a person the chance to catch his breath, relax and renew. Or ruminate on the mistakes he had just made in his last relationship. I let out my breath, pushed away thoughts of Vic and tried to focus on my book.

Ted made another pass on the mower and I watched the sweat roll down his back as he went by. He was handsome, tall and rangy with broad shoulders, wavy salt-and-pepper hair and large hands. His manner was laid back and friendly, his blue eyes bright and inviting.

The first morning, I had come down for breakfast at 9:30 as instructed. I could hear someone in the kitchen working with pots and pans and whistling. The smell of fresh-brewed coffee lured me through the swinging door and I stopped at the sight of Ted standing at a counter with his back to me. He wore a T-shirt and shorts with flip-flops, and his casual masculinity and good spirits made me wonder what it would be like to wake up beside him each morning. Much different from the mood swings and dour manner of Vic, I could bet.

He turned to grab a pan and smiled when he saw me at the door. "Good morning, Dave! How'd you sleep?"

He had invited me to sit and have a cup of coffee and I wound up eating with him at the butcher-block kitchen table rather than in the formal dining room. He told me the history of the Blue Goose Inn and some of the more unusual parties they had hosted, and after cleaning up the dishes, he excused himself to run some errands.

Now, Ted completed a third circle and I had to force myself not to look up from my book, even when the mower engine shut down. I read another paragraph, trying to remember the characters and situation. I was so focused on appearing absorbed in my book I didn't see him approach.

"I'm not disturbing you, am I?"

I jumped and looked up to find him standing at the edge of the patio, beads of sweat caught in the hair on his chest and grass clippings stuck to his ankles and muscular calves. I must have given him a blank look because he half turned and gestured at the tractor. "I'm not disturbing your reading, am I?"

I smiled, trying not to stare at his crotch. "Oh! No no, you're not disturbing me. It's kind of nice, actually, to see another person and hear some noise. It's so quiet and removed here, kind of makes me feel like we're the last two people on Earth."

"Yeah, it does take some getting used to," he said quietly, nodding and looking out over the lawn. "Imagine that: the last two people on Earth. You'd have to really like the other person, wouldn't you?" He looked back at me. "So, you on your own now?"

I blushed and ducked my head. "Does it show?" I looked up again and shrugged. "I was in a pretty long relationship, but I guess it ran its course. So, here I am on my own. Again."

Ted nodded. "I know what you mean. I'm feeling that way, too. My wife is out of town these two weeks and I'm kind of bouncing back and forth between, 'Hey, I'm free to do what I want,' and 'Hey, there's no one to talk to.'" He locked his blue eyes with mine a moment, his face suddenly serious. I looked back at him, drawn into his searing blue gaze, and then he gave me a small smile. "Do you have dinner plans?"

I smirked. "Well, last night I finished the granola bars and corn chips I brought with me, so I'm going to say whatever restaurant you can recommend that's not too far away."

"Care to join me for dinner? It's not a fancy place, but they make a good burger."

My stomach twisted pleasantly and I found myself nodding. "Yeah, that would be great."

Ted nodded once and clapped his large hands together. "Okay then. Be ready by six and meet me in the foyer."

"I'll be there. Thanks, Ted."

"Oh, no need to thank me," Ted said. "I hate to eat alone, too." He turned and walked back to his tractor and I watched his high, tight ass the entire way.

* * *

Ted took me to Bob's, a small, dark-paneled bar and grill that smelled of stale beer and decades of cigarette smoke and grease. We each ordered a burger with fries and a beer and made small talk until the food came. The burger was one of the best I had ever tasted and we talked as we ate, finding those small commonalities and building on them as strangers do. After finishing the food, we ordered a third round of beers and Ted flirted mildly with the waitress. When she walked away, he took a long pull from his beer, narrowed his eyes and asked, "You ever been in an open relationship?"

I took a drink to give myself time to consider my answer. "No, but some of my friends are, and they make it work."

"Yeah?" Ted took another drink. "I'm in one."

"Really?" I looked around the bar. "So you've slept with our waitress? Is that what you're saying?"

Ted laughed. "Bess? No, we just flirt with each other." He leaned a little closer. "But I have slept with her cousin, Richard."

I leaned forward and grinned at him as my cock stirred with interest at the sudden turn the conversation had taken. "Your wife lets you sleep with men?"

He leaned farther forward and grinned back. "Yep, because I let her sleep with women." He sat back and pulled out his wallet. "Ready to head back to the house?"

"Yeah, sure." I chugged the last of my beer and pulled out my wallet.

We split the bill and stepped out into the chill night air. Ted unlocked his truck and I climbed in beside him. It was an old pickup, the kind with a vinyl bench seat in front, and the dashboard lights highlighted the rounded bulge of his crotch.

We didn't talk much on the drive back to the house. I watched

the trees and cornfields flicker past in the wash of the headlights and tried not to think too much about Ted's sweaty, hairy
chest and tight, round ass. The air in the truck's cab seemed
to thicken with possibility, becoming more heavily charged as
Ted pulled slowly up the inn's gravel drive and parked by the
carriage house. He shut off the engine and we sat in silence for
a moment, the engine ticking as it cooled, and moonlight filling
the cab. Then he slid slowly across the bench seat and pulled me
into him. His lips were soft and his tongue tasted of beer and
burger. He put an arm around my shoulders, pulling me closer
still, and the heat pulsing off his body burned into me. His big
hands gripped me at shoulder and waist, holding me in place as
his gentle kiss turned more urgent.

He pulled back and looked at me, his eyes pale in the moonlight. "I hope this is okay with you."

"You have to ask?"

He smiled. "Good. It's been a long time since I've connected
with someone like this."

I pulled him back for another kiss and unbuttoned his
flannel shirt to run my hands through the hair on his chest. I
thumbed his nipples and he groaned into my mouth. He pulled
up my sweatshirt and ran his big, warm hands over my torso,
his fingers combing through the hair and pinching my nipples.

"I was hoping you'd have a hairy chest," he murmured as
he nuzzled my neck. "I wish I could see if you were a natural
redhead."

"I guess you'll have to wait until daylight for that," I replied,
and we both chuckled before his mouth covered mine again.

I knew we weren't leaving the truck until each of us had
come; we both needed release that quickly. We unzipped each
other's jeans and fumbled our cocks free of underwear, then I
lay on my back across the seat and Ted stretched out above me,

his hips over my face. His cock, long and solid with a fat, burly head, slid into my throat. I felt the hot embrace of his mouth on my cock and grunted as I sucked him. Ted's hips started slow but quickly picked up speed until he was fucking my face outright. Every now and then he would bury his cock completely in my mouth and his balls, soft, furry orbs of heat, rested across my nose. I breathed in the smell of him, the fresh scent of his body wash mixed with sweat, and swooned a little.

I came first, grunting a warning so that Ted took my dick from his mouth. He wrapped a big paw around my spit-slick shaft and stroked me to climax. I felt the hot splash of come across my belly, and then Ted's cock pulled out from between my lips. He hung over me in the moonlight, one hand supporting him on the seat and the other pumping fast along his prick. His balls swung above me and I lifted my head to suck them.

"Oh, fuck yeah," Ted gasped. "Suck my balls. Oh, that's good. Oh, fuck that's good." He groaned as he came and I felt his semen mix with mine.

Ted caught his breath and then kissed me for a moment before opening the driver's door and easing himself out. He pulled up his jeans but left his shirt unbuttoned as he rounded the truck to open my door. I started to sit up, but he held me down with one hand while he rubbed the thinning puddles of our cum into my skin.

"Semen is supposed to be a rejuvenating agent," he said and squeezed a few more drops of cum from my softened cock.

"Well, shit," I replied, "with all my masturbation, my stomach should look great when I'm in my seventies."

We laughed and he helped me out of the truck and we headed up to my room, the one he called the Duck Blind. It was decorated with duck wallpaper and mossy-green carpet. Green and blue plaid shams covered the pillows which Ted threw to the floor. He tore the comforter and sheet from the bed then turned to kiss me as we undressed. We were both hard again, our cocks dueling in time with our tongues.

Ted lay on his back across the bed and I knelt on the floor between his legs. I stroked his cock, sticky with drying cum, and sucked his big, furry balls. I eased Ted's legs up little by little until I had exposed his furrowed pink anus cloaked beneath a veil of downy hair. The crack of his ass was damp with sweat and I paused to breathe in his scent before drilling my tongue into his twitching hole.

"That's it," Ted groaned as I feasted on his ass. "Oh, yeah, eat my ass. God, it's been a long fucking time since someone's rimmed me. Get your tongue in there deep."

I slurped, licked and sucked at his trembling sphincter while my cock bobbed in time with my pulse and a long strand of precum formed a puddle on the carpet.

Ted suddenly sat up, his legs coming down on either side of me. He grabbed me by the shoulders and lifted me up to kiss me hard on the mouth. He held me tight against him and lay back across the bed, our cocks grinding together and smearing us both with precum.

Rolling me onto my back, Ted slid down between my legs and took my hard cock in his mouth. He grabbed the loose skin of my nuts and pulled it taut then snaked a finger down to probe at my asshole. He sucked and probed and I groaned, my head twisting back and forth as his finger penetrated deeper and deeper.

Finally, I raised my head and said, "I want you inside me."

Ted raised his eyes and gave me a serious, promising smile. "I was hoping you would say that." He practically ran into the bathroom and I heard a couple of drawers open and close before he emerged, holding up a box of lubricated condoms. "We leave these in all the bathrooms, just in case."

I laughed. "Just in case you find someone to fuck?"

Ted gave me a narrow-eyed look but laughed as he peeled open the foil. "No. In case a guest is not as prepared as he or she should have been." He rolled on the condom and stepped between my legs, lifting them up to rest my calves over his broad shoulders.

"Are you ready?" he asked.

"Oh, yeah," I replied.

He leaned down and kissed me as the meaty head of his cock pushed past my sphincter. I opened my mouth to gasp and he caught the sound with his tongue. He paused a moment, pushed a little deeper into me, then a little more. Ted took his time until, finally, he lay on top of me, his tongue filling my mouth and his cock buried in my ass. I ran my hands over his back and down to the tight, hairy mounds of his ass where I clasped them hard and held him inside me.

A moment later, he pulled his hips back and his cock eased out. It nearly vacated me completely, but he shifted direction and plunged in again, pushing a grunt from between my lips. He fucked me then, hard and fast, his cock driving deep, stretching my hole and spanking my prostate. I grabbed fistfuls of the sheet beneath me and rode his cock until I felt myself getting close. I tried to hold on but his cock was angled just right and I finally reached down to jerk myself to climax. A jet of semen splashed up to my face and at the sight of my orgasm, Ted stood up and grabbed my ankles in his big, warm hands.

"Oh, fuck yeah," he moaned as he pounded into me. "I'm gonna fuckin' come. Oh yeah, I'm...oh, god!" His eyes squeezed shut and he grunted as his jizz filled the condom deep inside of me.

Ted slowly pulled out and stripped off the condom then collapsed on the bed beside me. We were sweaty and out of breath and he pulled me to him, pressing my sticky torso right up against his side.

"Wow," I said, not sure what else to say.

"Yeah," he replied. "Wow."

We lay quiet for a time, then I smirked and asked, "You're still going to make me breakfast tomorrow, right?"

Ted looked at me for a moment, and then we both laughed.

"Yeah, I guess you've earned it," he said. "But tomorrow night, we're staying in the Throne Room."

I felt a little thrill at the implication that he was staying with me that night and each night after. "The Throne Room?" I rose up on an elbow. "What's that?"

Ted shrugged. "Just another room in the house." He turned and kissed me softly. "I want to fuck you in every room of this house the next two weeks. By the time you leave here, you won't remember the name of the asshole you broke up with."

I smiled and lay my head on his cooling chest. "That would be nice."

"And tomorrow you can help me clean out the gutters."

"What?" I exclaimed as Ted laughed. I playfully smacked his chest and sucked hard on his nipple before pressing my cheek against his chest again.

Maybe this time to reflect and relax hadn't been such a bad idea after all.

GRAY AREA

Rob Rosen

The tour was scheduled for late that morning; first time I'd seen the property, or any of their properties for that matter. They were, in fact, offering my company an incredible corporate rate, and my boss wanted me to check it out, all first-hand like. Job perks: free lunches and time away from my desk. Oh, and the dudes in hotel sales are always hot. Chuck was no exception. Scratch that, Chuck was exception*al*. And straight. Guess nobody's perfect. But I'm getting ahead of myself here.

"Glenn," I said, in greeting, eyes glued to his stunning blue peepers.

"Chuck," he said, hand outstretched. "Welcome to the Hotel Grand."

My body trembled upon contact. I quickly glanced down and spotted the absence of a wedding ring. Still, my gaydar was reading near zero, a veritable flat-liner. Bummer. Though there was some sort of blip there. Maybe it merited investigation. "Eager for the show," I replied, dripping with double entendre.

Not that he noticed. "Great, let's get going, then we can have lunch. On the house, of course."

You bet your sweet ass, emphasis on the sweet, I thought, but said, instead, "Oh, that's very generous of you. Can't wait."

And then we were off. It was, by all accounts, a pretty standard hotel. Very Courtyard Marriott without the name recognition. Still, the rate they were offering at all of their fifty statewide locations was unbeatable. Meaning, with or without the tour, I'd be signing a deal with them. Chuck, of course, was just icing on the cake. And what a yummy fucking cake it was.

First stop were the grounds: manicured lawns, outside heated pool, even a fire-pit. All while Chuck gestured wildly, arms outstretched, coated as they were in a thick, brown down. I smiled and nodded all the while, his deep voice rattling inside my chest, my own voice fairly lodged in my throat. "Beautiful, isn't it?" he asked, before we reentered the hotel, his smile almost manic. Then he chuckled. "Sorry, too much coffee this morning."

I shrugged. "No prob. Long night last night?" In truth, I much preferred hearing about him rather than his boring chain hotel.

He nodded, smile still perma-frozen to his impossibly handsome face. "First date. Her appendix almost ruptured."

Now *that* I had to laugh at. "Almost?"

"Made it to the hospital just in the nick of time. It was hours before I could reach anyone on her cell that could come to my rescue." He sighed, nervously tapping his foot all the while. "I've always hated first dates. Now I know why." Again he paused, eyes suddenly locked with mine, a swarm of butterflies released inside my belly. "You a married man, Glenn? Lucky enough to be out of the horrible rat race?"

I coughed. "Um, no. Can't."

He led me back inside, furry arm accidentally brushing mine as he went past, those butterflies all aflutter. "Can't?" he asked, confused. "Parents won't let you?" Now it was his turn to laugh.

I ended that right quick. "As in government can't. Gay can't. Illegal can't. Like murder or drug smuggling."

The door hit him in the ass, causing him to jump. His face, while still beguiling, was now scrunched up. "Sorry. Me and my big mouth." He tugged uneasily on his ear. "Soon enough it'll be no big deal, I'm sure."

I nodded. "So they say. Whoever *they* are."

He changed the subject. "Okay then, how about the gym and sauna next?" He led me down a hallway, pointing out the two nice-sized meeting rooms, all at my company's disposal, should we need them. At a reduced rate, of course. Nothing's free. Except maybe the tour. And lunch.

Then we reached the gym. Well, gym-lite, at any rate. Place was small, some exercise bikes, old Nautilus equipment, those big bouncy balls that are all the rage these days, a TV turned on to CNN. There was a sauna, a small steam room, a dry sauna, and one indoor Jacuzzi big enough for four if the four were supermodel skinny.

Place wasn't empty either. There was one naked guy in the dry sauna—young, twenties, hung like a mule—causing an instant boner in my slacks. The other was in the Jacuzzi, also young, probably a friend of mule-dick, broad chest, thick nips, man-scaped; he gave a smile up at us, followed by a nod. We said our hellos and good-byes all at once.

"Sorry," Chuck apologized. "Place is usually empty this time of day." A flush of red made its way up his neck.

"What?" I couldn't help but ask. "Uncomfortable with the

naked dudes? Can't take me to see the girl's sauna?" The blush spread across both cheeks. It was easy enough to read between the lines. "Ah," I added, with a knowing nod. "Uncomfortable with the naked dudes and the gay guy. Got it. No sweat."

We were in the hallway now. He stopped walking. "No, it's not that, it's just..." He paused, a nervous smile going northward on his face. "Okay, maybe a bit. I'm sorry."

I grinned. "Nothing to be sorry about. I get it. And, to be fair, I *was* checking them out. Hard not to, really." Then it was my turn to pause, also with a nervous smile. "Don't straight guys check each other out, too? Comparing notes, I mean. Isn't that just human nature?"

The nervous smile was replaced by a nervous chuckle, the sound like ice tinkling in a frosty gin and tonic, which, right about then, I was feeling I could use. We continued walking. "I suppose so," he replied. "Like you say human nature. Curiosity killing the cat."

The business center was next on our tour: basically, a small room with a couple of computers and a fax machine. We just peeked in. I was sure he would've liked me to drop the conversation, but I pressed on, nonetheless. Curiosity, as he put it, was yanking on my cat's collar. Hopefully, it wouldn't choke it to death. "You know, even if the saunas were coed, I would've checked out the ladies, too. I mean, I may be on a diet, by I can still look at the menu."

He turned, eyes locking with mine, a warm volt riding down the length of my spine. "Really?" he asked. "No way."

"Why not? Not like I've never been with a girl before. Drunken nights in college. These things happen. Life isn't always so black and white, Chuck. Sometimes there's a gray area."

He walked me down the hall, pressing the elevator button, both of us now staring straight ahead. "Gray area, huh?" he said, voice suddenly shaky. "I can see that."

The doors opened. We stepped inside. He pressed the button to the top floor. "You, uh, you ever have a gray area, Chuck?" I watched his reflection in the highly polished doors. He winced, just slightly, the gaydar blip suddenly spiking.

"No, not really," he replied.

"Not really as in *no*, or not really as in *sort of*?" I couldn't help but ask, with a sudden stirring in my slacks.

The elevator stopped, and we got off and started walking down the hallway to what I guessed was one of their nicer rooms. They always show you the nicer ones. Then I hear the complaints from my coworkers when they get stuck with a first-floor unit that's right by an elevator shaft. "Oh, you don't want to hear about it," he told me. "Happened forever ago. It was nothing, really."

We stopped at the door to the room he was planning on showing me. "C'mon now, Chuck. Spill."

He just stood there. Sighed. Room card in mid-swipe. "One night I caught my college roommate jacking off. Came home late and he was watching porn. He couldn't flick it off fast enough, so he left it on."

The image flashed through my head, vividly, my cock now hard as granite. "Let me guess. You were drunk. You watched it with him. Long story short, you both jacked off watching it. Close?"

He swiped the card and we went inside, the door locking behind us, *click*. "Exactly," he replied. "Right on the nose. No big deal."

I patted him on the back. "Yep, no big deal, dude. Horny teenager shit."

He exhaled and laughed again. "Exactly." Then another pause. "All three times."

I coughed. "In one night?"

"No, of course not. Three times that semester. Then we graduated and I never saw him again."

And that was the end of that. Or so he thought. He showed me the room, the amenities, the view, and then he excused himself to go to the restroom. By the looks of things, and the sweat that had been forming across his brow, I think poor old Chuck wasn't prepared to be spilling the beans, as it were, to a complete stranger and a gay one at that.

I sat on the king-sized bed and held the remote. I'd been in my fair share of hotel rooms before. I knew the drill and found what I was looking for quickly enough. *Debbie Does Detroit* was already flashing across the giant, flat screen as he emerged. That nervous chuckle of his made its triumphant return. "Ha ha, very funny, Glenn."

I looked up at him with a sly wink. "Something to lighten the mood." I turned and looked at the screen again. "But there is one thing I don't get, Chuck, about straight porn."

Now he was watching, too, an anxious tic lifting up his right eyebrow. "What's that?"

I scratched my head. "It's full of, well, *dick*. Big, hard dicks. Isn't that distracting for you?" I asked. "I mean, you throw a naked woman into a gay flick and that scene is gonna be fast-forwarded straight on through, guaranteed."

"You, um, just ignore it. It's like a prop, really."

I nodded, staring at the screen, where Debbie was blowing a donkey-dicked dude at that very moment. "That's one big prop," I made note. "Hard, pardon my choice of words, to ignore."

He shrugged. "That's what lesbian porn is for then," he managed, pulling at his shirt collar. The air-conditioning wasn't on. Poor guy was sweating something fierce. "So, how about that lunch?"

I pointed at the screen. "Yeah, sure, but can't we wait until the, um, *climax*, so to speak? Might as well get my money's worth." I scratched my head again. "Well, the next person's money's worth, at any rate."

He forced a smile and sat down at the far corner of the bed. "Sure, I guess so," he relented. "They both *climax* in about a minute, anyway."

My heart went pitter-patter. I'd caught him, and he knew it. "So you've seen this before, huh? Don't tell me you take breaks up here, Chuck?" I looked over at him with a mischievous grin. "I guess you can wipe the bill clean whenever you like, right?"

The blush returned, the tic a second later, sweat dripping down his cheek. "You know how it is," he confessed. "Stress reliever."

I nodded, upping the ante. "You look mighty stressed right now."

Again he fiddled with his collar, a quick wipe of sweat off his face. "Please tell me you're not suggesting we jack off together, Glenn. This isn't college, it's not late and we're not drunk. And I'm straight, need I remind you?"

I nodded, trying to keep my voice even. "Suddenly I'm not all that hungry. I kicked off my loafers and pushed my ass in reverse, sliding onto the bed, until I was leaning against the pillows against the backboard. Then I patted the space next to me. "I promise not to tell." Which could've meant that I promised not to tell his supervisors that he jacked off on company time or that I wouldn't tell anyone that he'd jacked off with me. Meaning, he knew he could be in trouble.

Still, I played it innocent. He was, after all, a nice guy. And stressed, for sure. In need of some relief. "Besides, Debbie already got off the donkey-dicked dude. Now she's on to the auto mechanic. Gotta see what happens next, Chuck; I'm invested." Slowly, I unbuttoned my shirt, yanking out the material tucked into my slacks, my chest and belly quickly revealed, lungs madly expanding and contracting by that point. Then I patted the bed again.

He stood, the frame creaking. Then he walked to the air controls and flicked on the unit, a nice cool breeze flowing over us within seconds. Thank goodness for Chuck, who now had two massive pit stains, his back a sopping mess, shirt clinging to him in all the right places. Not that it stayed on for much longer.

He didn't speak or look at me. He kicked off his dress shoes, then unbuttoned his shirt, untucking it as I had mine. I watched in awe as his chest was revealed, so thick with fur you could barely see the tanned flesh beneath, then a belly etched with muscle, also rising and falling in double-time. The shirt was removed and slung over a chair. "Too bad for you, Glenn," he squeaked out. "Next scene is one of those lesbian ones."

I grimaced and unbuttoned my slacks, reaching my hand in to grab my throbbing cock. "I might have to keep my eyes closed." Or divert them to my side, more than likely.

"So much for that gray area, Glenn," he chided, unhooking his belt, then popping open his top button. Zipper came down next, *ziiip*. His slacks fell to the ground, were kicked off then got slung over another chair, leaving him in a snazzy pair of silk boxers, a mild tent dead center, a noticeable wet spot, too. He watched as I shimmied out of my slacks, my briefs at full mast, the space next to me beckoning. He sighed and hopped on, three inches from me, nothing touching, both our eyes glued to the screen. Debbie finished off the mechanic, a trail of spooge dripping down her chin. Thankfully, the sound was muted; I think it would've been more than I could handle.

I glanced over at Chuck. His hand was in his boxers, fiddling with his junk. I took that to mean that all systems were go, and I pushed down on my briefs, kicking them off, my dick swaying as I got comfortable again. Chuck's eyes remained glued to the screen; still, he echoed my maneuver and was naked soon enough, both of us in nothing but our black socks now.

I glanced down the length of him, muscle and wiry hair for days, boulder-like calves, big-ass feet, hairy knuckles. His hand was wrapped around his prick, which I still wasn't brave enough to peek over at yet. Then again, I had one more weapon in my arsenal to help remedy that. "Um, I forgot to ask you, Chuck," I started, clearing my throat. "That roommate of yours, did you jack each other off or just go at it solo?"

His head turned my way, those eyes of his big and bright. "I was afraid you were going to ask that."

It was then that I got a gander at my heart's delight. He'd let go of his prick. It stood at attention, six inches, sausage-thick, the head wide as a plum, slick with precome. "Dude turned out queer, didn't he?" I asked.

"As a three-dollar bill," he answered. "And, yes, we jacked each other off. But that was all."

Tentatively, I reached over. His eyelids fluttered upon contact, my hand wrapped tight around his hefty tool. "So you won't mind this then?" I asked, the horse clearly already out of the barn. He moaned his reply; eyes still shut tight, hands now behind his head, the faintest of smiles creeping up his face. With little left to lose and a whole hell of a lot to gain, I asked, "Is there, uh, *anything* else you'd like me to do?"

His eyes popped open, the smile growing wider. "Well, since you're offering," he said, voice husky, cock pulsing in my grip. He hesitated, that cute blush of his returning. "I like um...my butt played with. Only, I can never ask a girl to do that."

My smile echoed his as I released my stroke and lifted up

his legs, hairy ass raised up, hair-haloed hole winking out at me. "Lick it or just finger it?" I asked, all eager beaver, pardon the expression. "Both would be nice." A gross understatement if ever I'd heard one.

Talk about your rare delicacies: straight ass. I leaned in and down, taking a deep whiff, musk and sweat filling my nasal cavities. I gave my cock a tug, come already rising from my balls. Then I dove in, face-first, my tongue lapping his crinkled ring, sending a groan down from his mouth that made the entire bed shake. It grew louder as my tongue deftly shoved its way inside, all while I stroked my cock with my left hand, his cock with my right, his heavy, hairy balls bouncing on my forehead. "Fuuuck," he rasped, deeply, the sound swirling around my head.

"Getting to that," I mumbled into his ass, sucking and slurping on his asshole. Then I leaned back and hocked a loogie at it, saliva dripping down his crack before I handed his tree-trunk-thick cock back over to him, seeing as my hand would now be busy. He gladly took it, beginning a slow stroke as he eagerly eyed my progress.

I spanked his hole with my index finger and its shorter neighbor, then gently, slowly, tenderly inserted their tips, then the digits up to the knuckle. He sucked in his breath, his hole clenching around the intruders. I waited. He exhaled and relaxed his grip, hand speeding up around his meat, balls bouncing. I shot him a wicked grin as I watched all this, my hand gliding its way up his tight hetero ass.

With both fingers now entrenched deep within, I gave them a jiggle, feeling the smooth, muscled interior of him. Then I let him have it, slow at first, then power-pumping his rump, both of us keeping up the rhythm on our cocks until I felt his prostate grow rock hard.

His hirsute body tensed just before he erupted, cock quivering in his grasp, thick bands of come spewing out, dousing his belly and chest. His asshole gripped my fingers like a vise; still, I had my free hand, which was pistoning my prick, lightning fast. A second later, I shot as well, gobs of spunk that splattered all over the hotel comforter, which is why you're never supposed to sit on them, as they rarely get washed.

Both of us were moaning and groaning now, bodies twitching as every last ounce of come got shook out. Then I retracted my fingers and collapsed next to him, our chests rising and falling as we tried to catch our breaths. Our little corner of heaven, room 603.

"Great hotel you have here," I quipped.

He laughed. "We aim to please, Glenn."

I stared at the puddles of spunk that had amassed around his midsection. "Your aiming is impeccable, Chuck." I turned and stared up at the ceiling, a wave of relaxation washing over me. "One last question, though. Then lunch, because suddenly I'm starving."

He groaned. "Fine. But last one."

I nodded. "No prob, dude. It's just, um, those three times with the college roommate…"

Again he laughed, turning his head in my direction. I looked over as well, drowning in those pools of blue. "Did I say three, Glenn? Maybe it was more like eight. Who can say no to a free blow job?"

I reached over and slapped his chest. "You never mentioned any blow jobs, Chuck."

He smiled, jumped up, and came back with two damp towels. "Didn't I?" He wiped down his fur, cock swaying to and fro. "Now you see why I can offer you such great rates, Glenn."

I snapped my fingers. "You scratch my back, I blow your dick?"

He touched finger to nose. "Bingo, Glenn. It's pretty black and white, if I do say so myself."

I laughed hard. And my cat, praise be, was no longer the least bit curious.

EPIPHANY

Jamie Freeman

Jacksonville, Florida, 1952

I park the '48 Buick down the street at an all-night diner where there are enough customers at the counter and cars in the lot to provide some camouflage for her while I'm gone. She's a black four-door sedan that looks like just about every other car on the road, almost four years old, but well taken care of, washed on weekends and waxed once a month. My father-in-law bought the car wholesale, decided he wanted a flip top and sold it to me for next to nothing. Susan insists he didn't do it out of pity. She's right; it was pride. The old man couldn't stand the thought of his baby girl riding around in a rusted-out pickup truck when his face is up on billboards all over town trying to put a shiny new Buick in every garage in Jacksonville. But there was no way I was gonna be able to afford a new Buick, not on a junior salesman's salary, so I guess it's all right with me that he suddenly got generous.

I duck my head, shove my hands in my pockets and cross the parking lot. I slip around the back of the diner into an alley that smells like piss and old beer and rotting garbage. The Florida night is hot and wet and I'm sweating like a pig by the time I cover the three blocks to the door of the bar.

There are half a dozen bikes standing outside, mostly Harleys including a couple of those new chromed-up Hydra-Glides. When I get close enough to the bikes, the smell of sweaty leather slaps me hard, bringing my rod to rigid attention. I move my fingers around in my pockets and rub my cock, getting a nice strong erection going under my khakis before I step inside.

The place is dim but loud with the blare of the jukebox, the clatter of pool cues and the low hum of male voices. Laughter punctuates the sounds, a particularly loud, baritone thunder rumbling up from a fat guy with a cigar butt stuffed between his teeth. He's a bit-part player right out of an old movie, drying glasses with a dirty gray rag then wiping the sticky bar with the same rag. He looks up at me and says, "Whiskey?"

I nod, sidle up to the bar, and pull out a pack of Salems.

The bartender slams my glass onto the bar in front of me and I pass him a buck. He's back with change before I can light my cigarette.

I light up and take a long drag, letting the smoke filter down into my lungs, expunging the memory of a day full of pacing and fake-smiling and ringing up sales at the men's clothing store where I'm currently serving time. Susan says I'm lost and when I find myself I'll suddenly become a success. There are so many things wrong with that statement I can barely get a handle on all of them, but I guess at least she's trying to defend me, or maybe she loves me, or maybe she just defends me out of habit. Her daddy the other day, when he thought I couldn't hear him through the jalousie windows, though I'm maybe ten fuckin' feet away from the man, pushing that damn push mower back and forth in a silent patchwork, he said I'm shiftless. That's the word he used: shiftless. And I imagined shoving him down in the grass and rolling the mower over him, letting the round blades chop him into mulch that would probably poison everything in the yard.

I take a long slow sip of the whiskey, letting the liquor burn across my tongue and down into my gullet, spreading a warm, floaty calm all through my body.

My boss says I've got an anger problem. I tell him, "I ain't got no anger problem, Dave; it's just that the world's full of fuckin' idiots." He just rolls his eyes at me when I talk like that 'cause he knows I'm just proving him right. We've known each other since high school so he knows my history, knows about my war record, my useless high school diploma and honorable discharge papers, and of course, my temper.

The last night before we shipped out for North Africa back in '42, me and Dave went out to this little dive bar over at the beaches where he knew a girl who he said could get us cheap liquor and free blow jobs. I figured I'd have to use my "I'm shipping out tomorrow; it'd be terrible to die a virgin" line, but we get there and the girl—Sarah or Sandra or something—slides us a bottle of whiskey across the bar and says, "It's on the house, boys." So me and Dave take turns drinking and watching a couple of skinny girls sitting together at a table in the corner and fanning themselves with paper fans.

Pretty soon Dave gets up and ambles over to them, pulling up a chair and sitting backward on it, arms resting on the curved back, eyes glued to these two dolls, and he motions me over, so

I bring over the bottle and sit down. Even the burning blur of the alcohol couldn't hide the fact that these two were homelier in person than they were from across the bar. The girl closest to me leaned back so her face was half hidden in shadow, but her profile was long and horsey and her lips were red and heavy. They were cocksucking lips; lips too dull and dense to make conversation, but amply constructed for the only thing I wanted from her.

So we pass around the bottle and Dave takes the lead. When the bottle's getting near to empty, he says, "How 'bout it?" Just like that, and the girls get up, skirts swishing as they move, and they pass us and head for a door behind the bar. I'm on my feet, holding on to the bottle and stumbling through the tiny room packed to overflowing with empty chairs. My cock is already hard when Dave pushes open the door and we see the two girls, standing on opposite sides of the shadowy room. There's a little window up high on one side of the room, and there's a little light seeping in through the smudged dust and dirt, but other than that the room's dark. I head over to my girl and the door closes behind us, slamming us into near complete darkness.

I feel her hands on my pants and in a flash her cool, skinny fingers are sliding up and down my cock. I grab her hair and push myself into her mouth, a deep-throated grunt punctuating the silence and making me grin a little. Her mouth is tight and hot and she knows exactly what she's doing, sliding up and down, testing techniques and sticking to the ones I react to. The heat in the room is unbearable. I slide my shirt up and push the fabric over behind my head, the tight cotton pulling against my arms but exposing my stomach, chest and pits to the air. And she's working me over, her mouth pulling me through my drunkenness to sobriety and then pulling me one step farther into orgasm. I come in her mouth, holding the back of her head when she squirms, letting her suck me until the waves of sensation have passed.

I push her back off my tool, but her center of gravity shifts and she topples backward. I reach out my hand: "Give me your hand," I say. She doesn't say anything. "Give me your fuckin' hand," I say, getting louder and leaning forward to snatch her up off the ground.

She's up, trying to stand and suddenly my hand moves forward and I end up with this long skinny cock in my hand, oozing come all over my fingers.

"What the fuck? *What the fuck?*"

I'm seeing red by this time, and I yank hard on that cock. The doll-boy screams, his voice shrill and high. "Leave me alone," he shouts, and that's when I wail on him. I'm seeing red and pounding on him with both fists and Dave's yelling and his girl or boy or whatever is shrieking too, this high-pitched, panicked sound and I'm still wailing this guy as hard as I can and I can smell the coppery odor of blood and that's the only thing that stops me.

"Fuck," I say.

"Get out of here! Get out of here!" Dave's girl is yelling over and over and then, "He ain't mean it. He ain't mean it."

And my blood's finally starting to settle, my arms are dropping slack and my head's clearing. And Dave pulls me out the door and pulls me running through the bar, turning over chairs and yanking me through the doorway and then I'm puking up my guts in the road, wave after wave of nausea exploding out of me like automatic gunfire.

And now Dave's shouting at me, "What did you do that for? What's your fucking problem?"

I don't say anything, just wipe my mouth with the back of my hand and feel a cold sense of panic in the pit of my stomach. And

I don't remember how we got home that night, or anything else until we got on the bus to go to the naval base, but I remember looking up into the streetlight, my eyes focused unblinking on the humming radiance and thinking I was a no-good-piece-of-shit-nobody just like my sainted father.

Tonight I'm still caged and angry, but I'm a decade farther along than that fucked-up kid who beat the shit out of a boy for giving him a free backroom blow job. Tonight I'm pacing my cage, looking for a fuck. Looking for a man to fuck me out of this horrible, boring life that I fought like a madman to defend in the burning sands of North Africa and the muddy fields of Germany; looking for a man to fuck me out of this faithless, loveless trap of a marriage that I fought so hard to win when I got home from the war. I take one last drag on my cigarette, and then crush out the remains in a tin ashtray, pushing it down hard like I'm trying to sink the butt into the metal, my thumbnail an angry white from the pressure.

I spin around on my stool and let my eyes slide from one end of the room to the other. The men playing pool are absorbed in themselves, buying each other drinks and passing money back and forth across the worn green felt when the balls disappear from the table. A skinny young thing in khakis, loafers and a white oxford stands next to the front door stirring his drink with his finger and pouting prettily. A couple of regular joes are sitting at the tables now, some of them smoking, others just staring into their drinks and waiting for the click.

I turn around and slap my empty glass on the bar, motioning for the bartender to pour me another one. "Hold yer horses," he says, pulling a huge plug of tobacco out of a sweaty, soiled pouch and folding it in under his lower lip.

On the jukebox some Negro singer replaces Rosemary

Clooney and sings something loud and sad that makes me want to drink myself into oblivion. When the bartender pours my whiskey, I down it and point to the glass. He hits me again and I savor the burn and the sad jazzy music and light another cigarette.

I smile a little bit, thinking what my son-of-a-bitch father would say if he could see me here, sitting on this stool listening to Negro music and watching fairies play pool. An officer in the Klan back in the day, he'd run more than his share of Negro businesses out of town and he'd had more than one Negro politician hauled out in the woods and beat bloody or worse. He died of a heart attack a couple of years ago, just curled up one afternoon on my mother's porch swing, the venom in his heart finally saturating his sluggish blood and swamping him in pain, then silence and rigor. And I thought I'd be free then, but the door to my cage never so much as rattled in the breeze of his earthly departure and I'm stuck here with Susan and her father, mowing the lawn and bringing home a paycheck that's already spent, and dreaming of the open road.

I started coming here because I'd heard about the place at work or on a bus or something, a place people all knew about but where nobody'd ever been. One afternoon I drove by, trying to think of what alibi I could use if someone spotted me here, this far from home and work. But nobody saw me and I didn't stop. I drove by a couple more times then finally stopped one night when I was late getting off work. I stopped because something caught my eye from the road. Among the Harleys and Triumphs and BMWs, and what looked a hell of a lot like a British Bown, there stood an old battered, olive-green Harley Liberator.

I pulled the car over to the curb and got out without thinking. I walked over to the bike and stood staring at the old thing, leather seat worn and torn, paint scuffed and pockmarked. It was a beautiful sight.

"Hey, man, didja have one during the war?" a voice said behind me.

I turned around and looked at the tall blond man in blue denim pants and a leather jacket standing by the unmarked metal door.

"Yeah, sorta," I said, then, "I kinda inherited mine outside of Aachen in '44."

"Ah," he said, nodding slowly, reeling a memory in from a long way off. "Infantry, huh? First Army? I was with a bomber squadron trying to take out the infrastructure before you boys rolled into town."

"A pilot?" I asked.

"Navigator," he said.

"So where'd ya get the bike?"

"Bought it surplus when I got back to the States," he said, grinning.

About an hour later, we were five miles out in the country on a deserted dirt road and I was bending over with my pants shoved down around my ankles, hands braced on the cracked leather of the bike seat, and he was spit-fucking me into next week.

But god almighty that Harley was a beauty. There was something about those bikes—nothing like 'em on the battle-field really—and when you heard them coming or when you saw that driver sling his leg up over the bike and pull off his leather helmet, you knew there was something mythic going on here. Like Mercury, and not the pretty, girlish face on the old dimes, but a rugged warrior messenger. We were on the front lines of the greatest battle mankind had ever faced, fighting inch by muddy inch to free the world from evil, and these guys kept us alive and connected to whatever it was out there we were fighting for. These guys were our lifeblood and sometimes, our personal saviors. I rap my glass on the counter again and light another Salem. The swish in khakis has made his way over to the bar, perching on the edge of his seat and blowing smoke in my general direction. I look down at the dark wood grain beneath the thick coating of varnish, tracing the lines that branch out across the bar like a map to nowhere.

It was October 1944 and I'd been transferred from North Africa to Italy and then on to the German front. I was serving in a makeshift squad assembled after fighting the day before had left a dozen of us orphaned. We were pinned down in the woods somewhere outside Aachen, moving slowly, relentlessly toward the first big German city. Resistance was pretty stiff and we'd been bogged down along this stretch of forest for the better part of two weeks.

I was talking to the Squad leader when a couple of incoming shells burst right in front of us. His body flew at me under the force of the explosion and before I knew what was happening I could hear small arms fire and the sound of commands being shouted in German. I grabbed my rifle and hit a dead run in the direction of the nearest cover, launching myself over a fallen tree and rolling around, trying to get a bead on somebody who looked like a Kraut.

I found one, aimed my rifle through the shield of branches and watched the bullets rip into the face of a tall blond boy who had been running in my direction. He crumpled in a shower of aerosolized blood and his companion dove for cover, then started crawling across the leaves toward his buddy, giving me time to scramble up and run like hell.

I ran about a quarter mile before I realized my leg was gushing blood. My pants were shredded around an ugly flesh

wound and my boot was filling up with blood. I cursed and
started rummaging through my pack for something to use to
bandage the wound. A bullet whizzed past my head embedding
itself in a tree behind me. I looked up and thought I was going
to die there in the forest. A German soldier jumped through
a thick stand of shrubbery, running toward me full tilt, then
stopped short, flew back heels overhead and smashed into the
mud not two yards from my boots.

I looked behind me and there was a huge, muscular, dark-
eyed soldier standing astride his motorcycle with a rifle raised
to his eye.

He dropped the gun into the riding holster and shouted,
"Let's get you outta here, Private!" and I ran like hell toward
the man and the bike. He started the engine, flipped the bike
around in a startlingly smooth motion, grabbed my hand and
pulled me unerringly onto the bike behind him.

"Grab my waist," he shouted, "sit close and keep your head
down."

I heard the roar of the engine and the ping of a bullet rico-
cheting off the back fender and we flew out of there.

Enemy grunts greeted us with a hail of bullets at every turn
that afternoon and by evening, it was clear the Krauts had
pushed past our lines and left us isolated from the main American infantry force.

We rode for a while and then found a winding dirt road that
tracked a muddy stream. We drove for half an hour before we
pulled off the road and the driver said "Okay, kid, get off; let's
take the bike down over there, then cover our tracks. I gotta
figure out what the hell we're gonna do."

I dismounted and we pushed the bike down a muddy slope
to what looked like a small overhang, but turned out to be
a shallow cave carved into the high bank of the stream and

abutting the water. I ran back and obscured our trail, then hurried back to find my savior leaning on his pack and lighting a cigarette, grinning in the dim moonlight. The cave was small; the motorcycle, even flush with one side of the cave, took up most of the space. I squeezed in, pulling my legs in behind me and arranging the brush to screen us from view. I sat close beside the stranger and pulled my knees up beneath my chin, breathing softly, exhausted.

"What's yer name, kid?"

"Adler, sir."

He laughed. "A Kraut?"

"My great grandfather was."

"Don't fuckin' matter noways," he said. "My name's Becker."

"Also a Kraut name," I said with a tired shrug.

"Yeah, ain't that irony? I don't know about you, but I don't feel very welcome in my homeland right about now."

I laughed at this and Becker lit a fresh cigarette off of his and handed it to me, the hairy muscles of his forearm flexing in the half light, his eyes never leaving mine.

"Well, Adler, we're gonna hunker down here for the night. I can't see how we stand a better chance riding around in circles wasting gas and bumping into German sentries in the dark than we do just hiding out here till first light." He took a long drag on his cigarette. "I got what's left of a K ration in my pack so nobody's gonna starve, at least not tonight."

"Okay," I said, looking up from my leg, my breath fogging in the cold winter air. The wound on my leg looked shallow and had pretty much stopped bleeding. If I could keep the mud out of it, I might be okay.

"You're hurt," Becker said, shifting onto his knees to have a look. The moon was low and bright in the sky, approaching fullness and shining down through the tree branches.

He turned my leg gently toward him, pulled back the bloody cloth and traced his finger along the edge of the wound. He crawled over to his bike, rummaged through his pack and came back with a first-aid kit and a canteen. He sat back down and pulled my legs gently over both of his, sitting with his back against the dirt-packed wall. I moved closer, letting him position me in the moonlight. He gently washed and dressed my wound, his hands moving quickly and competently. He looked up at me and caught me studying his face. I blushed like a sixteen-year-old girl.

"What?" he said, a half smile crossing his chapped lips.

"Nothing. Thanks for doing that," I said pointing to my leg.

"You got first watch," he said, eyes still watching me.

We ate in silence, splitting some canned meat, crackers, cheese and chocolate. It seemed like a feast compared to what I'd been eating the last few days. Becker spent some time after we ate staring at a folding map, trying to figure out where we were. When he finally gave up, he settled down in the cramped space, stretching his legs out and slumping down on his pack, his body stretched out close beside where I sat smoking another one of his Chesterfields.

"Adler?"

"Yeah?"

"You ever get horny out here in the woods?" he asked.

My heart jumped into my throat, beating so hard I was sure he could hear it in the confined space. My cheeks burned and I could feel a hard-on beginning inside my fatigues.

"No," I said evenly.

"Night then, kid," he said. "Wake me at oh-two-hundred."

He didn't move an inch, and I felt rather than heard him drift into sleep, his breath evening out and slowing, his features slackening.

I sat there and tried to stay awake, listening to the sounds of insects and frogs and the distant rumble of a bombing raid, like summer heat thunder back home. But my mind was cluttered with images I couldn't get rid of. All those moments when I questioned things came back to me suddenly. Listening to my bunkmates jerking off after lights-out on the troop transport ship; watching Grady pump himself behind the mess hall in that encampment near Biskra; all those muscled chests stripped down and tanned dark in the desert heat; or later, here in Germany, sleeping in my foxhole with my buddy Davison butt-up against me, shivering in the cold and his cock, hard as a rock rubbing against my ass. Some of it was just being thousands of miles from girls and being horny as hell, but there was something different for me. I could hear my father yelling at me, calling me a "fucking sissy" and beating the hell out of me when he found me and my cousin beating off in my grandfather's barn. I wanted him to be wrong. But I looked down at Becker's face and saw something that frightened me. His jaw was hard and stubbled and I wanted to run my fingers along his sandpapered cheek. I swept my eyes down his body. He was a mass of muscle, hairy and thick; just a huge, hulking guy. In the closeness of the cave, his body reeked of sweaty feet and armpits and ass, and that peculiar musk that could only be coming from between his legs.

I let my eyes slide down his stomach, across his belt buckle to the visible bulge in the front of his pants. I could see the long fat line of his erection under the olive drab.

I licked my lips and tried to look away.

"You all right, Adler?" His voice was gravelly, edged with sleep.

"Yeah, I'm just thinking," I said, dragging on the last bit of the cigarette, crushing out the butt reluctantly and holding the smoke captive in my lungs as long as I could.

"Did you come in your pants?"

"No," I said, my voice suddenly icy.

"Maybe you had an epiphany," he said.

"I told you I didn't come in my pants, you asshole," I snapped.

He laughed at this, but lay there with his eyes closed, completely relaxed.

That's when I reached out and touched the front of his trousers, sliding my hand along the length of his cock from tip to base. Something snapped in my head and suddenly things seemed clearer than they'd ever been before. Suddenly I knew what all those memories meant and, although I was terrified that my father was right about me, I was excited too. I felt the gorge rising in my throat as I undid the flies of Becker's pants. He shifted onto his back and helped me pull his cock out of his pants. I bent down without thinking, taking his ripe blunt-headed cock into my mouth. The taste was harsh and salty, but the smell drove me crazy and I let his hard cock slide as far back in my throat as I could stand then pushed myself farther onto him until I gagged. I held him inside for a moment then started sucking him, sliding him in and out, letting my teeth graze along the shaft. He moaned softly and slid his hands into my hair, guiding me gently back and forth into his own rhythm.

I sucked him for a while, just starting to get used to the feel of his big cockhead sliding against my tongue, the roof of my mouth and the back of my throat, when he said, "I'm gonna come." He started to pull out, but I grabbed his ass and pushed him into me as far as he would go. I bobbed my head back and forth until I felt him shoot into the back of my throat in a pumping stream of heat. I pulled back, letting the head of his cock slide forward trailing salty ooze across the length of my tongue. I held the tip between my lips and sucked him dry. He bucked and twisted on the cave floor, sweat pouring down his face, his eyes open now, dark distended pupils watching me intently.

When I finally released his cock from my mouth it had wilted to half its erect size.

He sighed and said, "That was swell, kid."

He turned on his side, tucked himself back into his pants and leaned on his elbow eyeing me quizzically. "What can I do for you in return?" he asked.

"Fuck me," I said, my voice trembling in the stillness.

And he did. Twice more before the sun came up, his huge cock tearing me open and forcing its way inside me, the smell of sweat and come and leather and mud in the cave nearly overwhelming.

At first light we started off in search of the rest of the First Army. We had made it to within a mile of the American encampment when a Kraut sniper shot Becker off the bike. We skidded across the road, each of us thrown in opposite directions. I pulled my pistol, but the sniper had faded into the forest. I ran to Becker, but he was dead when I got to him, a massive head wound bleeding out onto the cold asphalt. I took one of his dog tags and pulled his body to the side of the road. I sat with him for a long time before I could bring myself to get back on the motorcycle and drive toward the American lines.

Now I turn on my stool and see a big hairy mountain of a man pushing through the door from the parking lot. He looks around the room, his eyes slamming into mine and locking in place. He crosses the room and sidles up to the bar next to me.

He towers a full six inches taller than me, his chest broad and rock hard under his shirt. He orders a double whiskey, pays and turns to face me. I can smell the sweat coming up from his jeans and seeping out through the cotton fibers of his T-shirt. Heat radiates off him in waves that make me light-headed. I can feel my erection pushing against the bars of its cage.

"You want a ride?" he says, his voice low and dark. He turns and walks back out the door, knowing I'll follow him.

I gulp down my drink and head for the door. In the lot he's leaning against an old Harley Liberator. The body's painted a luminous midnight-black and the chrome shines in the moonlight.

"You coming?" he asks, reaching down to rub his cock through the coarse denim then turning to swing a gigantic leg over the bike.

"Almost," I say, walking over to him and mounting the bike behind him.

WINDOW OF OPPORTUNITY

Barry Lowe

What woke me up was the prick to my throat. Not that sort of prick, but the kind that drew blood. I felt the warm trickle down my chest.

"Where is she, cunt?"

I wasn't at all surprised to wake up and find my life being threatened. I'd never felt safe in this room. What did surprise me was opening my eyes to stare up into the snarling face of a shaven-headed murderer. Nor did I expect my cock to get hard when I briefly glimpsed his huge biceps and the do-it-yourself tattoos along his arms.

"Where the fuck is she?" he was screaming, his spit landing on my face.

I had no idea what he was talking about.

A sixth sense had told me not to take this ground-floor boarding house room, but it was all I could afford. There were few alternatives: I could succumb and move into a communal apartment or house share with a number of other impecunious

student types like myself. Or I could go back home and live with
my parents. Neither alternative appealed. I like my privacy. The
room itself was fine, although the furnishings were Spartan: a
three-quarter bed, a wardrobe and chest of drawers; what more
could a poor student want apart from the share kitchen down
the hall and a very share bathroom and toilet at the end of the
hall? Well, there was the airy side window that flooded the
room with light, which was the problem. It just happened to be
on the ground floor. It was invisible from the street because it
was down a passageway shielded by a rotting wooden gate that
was permanently locked. From the backyard, a number of leafy
bushes edged the passage mouth. It was an ideal entrance for
anyone with mischief on his or her mind.

The real estate agent assured me they'd never had any break-
ins but I learned later he'd been somewhat casual with the truth.
True, no one had ever broken into the four-story building since
it had become a boarding house aimed at the student and musician market because of the clubs and the university nearby, but
there had been one murder, unsolved, three suicides, five over-
doses, two-dozen thefts, and a partridge in a pear tree. The
list of tragedies was so long it might just as well have been a
Christmas carol.

But there were no break-ins. That meant all the other mayhem
had been inside jobs. I quickly installed a deadbolt on the only
door even though it was against house rules and could get me
thrown out. As an added measure, I drilled screw holes in the
window frames so the bottom window would open only far
enough that an arm could intrude. No way was a human body
gonna fit through that space. I suppose I should have taken all
those precautions from day one but, hell, security costs money
and that was something I did not have in great abundance.

At least I slept calmly once the locks and bolts were in place, safe, or so I thought. I woke up a hair's breadth from death, choking for breath, a grip of iron about my throat. The shaved-headed snarling belligerent whose face was inches from my own had substituted throttling for throat slitting. Less blood, I guessed.

"Okay, fucker!" he spat. "Where is she?"

If he actually wanted an answer rather than drowning me in his saliva, he'd have to let me go. I was already purple in the face, not my most attractive coloring, and I was in danger of passing out. He must have realized and released me. I gasped for air, taking huge gulps into my lungs. As my heart slowed from thumping against my ribs to merely terrified I looked at my tormentor.

Yep, he was precisely the sort of reason I didn't want to live at home and share with other students. This guy was hot in a way that meant if I had to die, the victim of murder, this is the kind of guy I would prefer to do it.

One of his gobs oozed down my cheek. My tongue snaked out to taste the salty mucous. I rolled it around on my tongue, and then swallowed it down. If the intruder saw me he gave no indication.

My throat felt like sandpaper when I rasped out, "Where's who?"

"Don't act like a dumb cunt with me," he snapped. "If I find out you're fuckin' her, I'll cut you up so fine they'll mistake your body parts for sushi."

"Okay, look. My name is Luke. I'm a student. I moved in here six months ago. I don't know who was here before me, I didn't ask, but I have been getting these letters addressed to a Kylie. Is that who you're looking for?"

"Where are the letters?"

I got up slowly, and he sprang back in case I was about to

attack him, raising the knife to chest level. "I kept them in case this Kylie chick called in to pick them up. I was gonna give it a few more weeks then mark them *Return to Sender*. They're on the table over there." He sat at my cheap laminated table and ill-matching chairs, keeping a wary eye on me as he spread the envelopes out in front of him.

"Don't try anything fucker, because I'll be onto you before you even reach the door."

He began searching through the pile, muttering threats. "If I find some other fucker has been writing to her he's dead meat."

I knew there was only one writer as all the correspondence was in the same handwriting and it was all marked from Long Bay Jail.

"You wrote those letters?"

"What's it to you," he said.

I shrugged. "How'd you get in here anyway?"

He snorted his derision. "You really think a couple of screws in a window frame as old as this shit heap could withstand a bit of force?"

I examined the window and saw the deep scour marks where the nails had splintered through the rotting window jamb. So much for security. I went and sat opposite the guy.

"You sure she's not here?" he asked, sounding thoroughly defeated.

"Take a look around. You see anything that looks even remotely like a chick lives here?"

He rifled through my closet and my drawers.

"Not that drawer," I yelled.

He smirked, thinking he was about to find proof that his Kylie was my secret lover.

"Why not, scared I might find something incriminating?"

He wrenched the drawer out, spilling the contents on the floor, jumping back in surprise.

"What the fuck?"

"I warned you."

"What is that shit?"

"What's it look like?"

"Sex toys."

"Give the man a prize." I went over to gather up the spill and hide it away again but he was too quick for me, grabbing one of the larger dildos.

"You use this on some chick? She must have a cunt like the Grand Canyon." He waved it around like a comedy prop.

Grabbing it from him, I stuffed it back in its hiding place and turned on him. "Listen up. There are no chicks. Not Kylie, not any female. I'm gay. The toys are for me. I like cock up my ass. Got it?"

"You shittin' me? No way could you fit that up your butt."

"Wanna bet?"

"Must hurt like hell."

"Yeah, well, with that one I need a bit of chemical assistance."

"Uh?"

He was as thick as two planks.

"Drugs."

"You got drugs?" he asked with more enthusiasm than he'd shown so far.

"Nothing much at present. Just poppers."

He seemed disappointed. "Gives me a headache," he said. "Got any grog?"

I opened the small fridge I'd smuggled into my room. Cooking was strictly forbidden anywhere in the boarding house except for the communal kitchen which was so rancid with mold, food scraps and toxic leftovers that even the cockroaches avoided it for fear of contracting food poisoning. Everyone cooked in their rooms, which meant we had to put up with the periodic memos slipped under our doors demanding we cease such activity immediately on pain of expulsion. These usually appeared after one of the smoke alarms had been triggered by burning toast. Solution? Simple. Most of us removed the smoke alarm batteries as soon as we moved in.

I handed over a half bottle of Jack Daniels and two glasses. He sat backward on the chair, at home with my alcohol, glaring at me.

"How long you in the...um...resort?" I asked when the silence was threatening to become lethal. He'd downed two glasses of bourbon, which seemed to make him more belligerent than mellow.

"How did you know I...?"

I tapped the return address on the front of his envelopes then poured myself a generous portion of liquor.

It was getting late. "You got anywhere to stay tonight?"

"Halfway house on the other side of the city. But I thought I'd be staying here with Kylie. Didn't expect she'd run out on me."

"If you like, you can stay the night 'cause it's getting late for public transport."

"I don't trust queers."

"You can sleep on the floor then."

"Remember, I got a knife."

While we polished off the remainder of the bottle he told me why he'd been sent away: two years for robbery with assault. He made no pretense of his innocence or that he was badly treated by the system. In fact, he thought he got off lightly. There was also no regret and it was obvious he'd be back to his old life as soon as he made contact with his underworld mates.

While it was fun ogling the fucker, I couldn't get him to talk about what happened after lights went out in prison or what happened to cute young twinks in the shower. When he clammed up about such activities I yawned, telling him I had to get to bed.

"You really queer, mate?" he asked.

"Totally."

"You sure you're not fucking Kylie and pretending you're queer to save your skin?"

The idea was so ludicrous, I laughed. "My cock has never seen the inside of a cunt. Truth be known, I'm the kind of queer who likes to be on the receiving end and Kylie sure doesn't have the necessary equipment."

He picked up on that in quite the wrong way. "How do you know? When did you see her?" He sure wasn't the brightest match in the box.

"For fuck sake lighten up, man. I didn't see her. She's a girl, right? Girls don't have cocks, right? Well, I love getting dicked up the ass."

"Don't it hurt?"

"Why, you thinking of trying it?"

I should have kept my smart-ass comment to myself. He was up off his chair waving the knife in my general direction, too drunk to know what he was doing, which made him infinitely more dangerous and more appealing.

"I'm no fuckin' queer, mate."

"I know you're not. That was a joke."

"So you know I'm not queer? How can you tell?"

I decided to lay it on thick.

"Just one look at you. You're one bad fucker. A man's man. The sort of guy that chicks fight over. The sort of man us poor queers worship but know we can't have. All we can do is look and dream about having a man like you pumping his dick into our throat, skull-fucking us into submission or raping our nelly assholes."

He smiled. "Yeah." Then adjusted his crotch.

He was quiet for a moment. I could almost hear the cogs of his brain, thinking. Planning.

"How about you let me watch you pushing that rubber thing up your ass. It'll remind me of Kylie. She liked to put on a show to get me off."

"I have to be in the mood for the large one and totally drug fucked. But I can accommodate the next size down."

"It's been two years, mate. Just me and my right hand and my imagination."

"You really wanna watch some filthy queer degrade himself in front of you by putting on a show, sticking I dunno what up his boy cunt so you can jerk your hard cock thinking of your girlfriend?"

I started slurring my speech so it sounded like I was as pissed as he was. Sounded less threatening to his fragile masculinity. I didn't doubt for a moment the guy was straight, but I knew about situational homosexuality and he must have played the game in prison at least once or twice. If I could keep him on heat he might at least let me watch him jerk his meat because that morsel between his legs seemed to be stiffening by the second.

"You got anything better I can watch?" he demanded. "Porn, that sorta shit?"

I didn't have a TV or a player, so he was out of luck there.

"I'd feel so fuckin' dirty knowing that a big hunk like you was watching me degrade myself. What choice do I have? You got a knife." I spoke softly, raising my voice several notches so I sounded more feminine. I minced over to the bedside table to switch on the lamp. "Honey, why don't you turn off the over-head so it's not so bright? That way I can put on a real good show for you. Here, make yourself comfortable." I plumped up a ratty cushion that had seen better days and pushed it to the back of the faded armchair that I had saved from a heap of furniture piled high on the footpath when one of the long-term residents had been locked out for nonpayment of rent. I moved it to the end of the bed so he would have a perfect view.

As I rummaged through my toy drawer for props and the bottle of lube, my hand brushed against an item I had long forgotten. I'd found it under the bed when I first moved in; obviously it had been the property of the absconded Kylie.

"You almost ready?" he snapped. Obviously the sexual tension was getting to him.

"Nearly there, honey."

He smiled. "I like it when you call me 'honey.' Reminds me of Kylie."

"Why don't you strip out of those clothes, honey. Get yourself real comfortable."

That idea made him extra uncomfortable. He fidgeted. "That shit you snort. Better give me some of that. Might help."

I took two small bottles from the fridge, giving him the unopened one. It should blow the top right off his head. The other would do me because I was so buzzed that I hardly needed artificial stimulants.

As I stripped off my T-shirt I heard the hiss of his poppers being opened, followed by a right old snort or two. If that didn't do the trick nothing would.

I heard him mutter, "Holy shit!" as he struggled to remove his old clothes, falling into the chair half undressed. I bent over to remove the boxers I'd been sleeping in ensuring that he got a good glimpse of my smooth hairless buns. While my head was lowered I opened the tube of lipstick that I'd found and applied it to my mouth. My hair was naturally longish—students can't always afford haircuts—and I hoped I looked sufficiently girly to pass in his frenzied state.

For a little extra courage I took a hit or two from my bottle and when I heard my heart pumping in my ears I stood up and turned to him.

His eyes opened to the size of saucers. "Shit, mate, you're fuckin gorgeous."

"Here, let me help you out of those uncomfortable old clothes of yours," I simpered as I kneeled in front of him, undoing the buttons on his shirt, taking the opportunity to flick each nipple, making him shudder. His body was wiry with scarcely any body fat. His muscles were pumped; obviously he spent a lot of time with weights while he was in prison. His arms carried the scars of inmate tattoos signifying gang allegiances and a crude sexual outline of a woman with big tits. The name Kylie was inked beneath it.

I held the poppers to his nose. "Here, honey. This will make you feel real good. Take a big sniff for Kylie."

Two snorts in each nostril and a beat or two before I leaned in to kiss the tat of Kylie. He groaned as I left the imprint of my lips. Then I turned my attention to his jeans. He'd managed to pull them partway down.

"Here, shift your ass, honey, so I can get you out of these pants."

He lifted up, allowing me to drag down his jeans and his stained briefs. His cock popped free, fully hard, oozing its impatience, a nice thick morsel just ripe for my throat. He was still high, so I quickly leaned in licked his cock slit, tasting his salty slime on my tongue.

He must have liked it because he kicked his trousers off fully to give himself more maneuverability before pushing two fingers inside my mouth, stretching my lips apart. I sucked each digit, tasting the grime of his past, eager to get back to his cock.

"Let me take care of you, honey," I said, pushing him gently back against the chair. I cradled his balls in my hand as I placed my red lips over his nipple and sucked, nipping it slightly with my teeth. I repeated the exercise on the other nipple, then traced my tongue down his chest toward his navel. It did the trick. He grabbed my head, moving it to his crotch. I opened wide and he plunged his prick straight down my gullet, choking me, which seemed to please him. "Suck it, bitch. Give my cock a good workout. First decent blow job I had in years."

His cock was a work of art and I could have sucked it all night. If that's all I got I'd take it and be well pleased. But what I wanted more than anything was to feel his rod pounding my butthole.

Keeping his hands on the back of my head, he pushed me down to his balls, stretching my throat around his cock, the lipstick smearing each time I slid up and down his slimy pole. I knew he wouldn't last long if he hadn't been getting a lot of action in prison, but I hoped he'd have enough in his balls for a backup session. I was counting on it.

"Oh, baby, your mouth is so fuckin' sweet," he cooed.

I lifted my face off his knob; his piss slit was leaking profusely. "Honey, you give me a mouthful of your hot man-spunk and after I swallow it right down, you can plug my tight cunt hole with this big pole of yours."

"You fuckin' swallow? Oh shit. I wanna see that."

I spit-bathed his cock until my drool was running down all over his balls, but I didn't dare play with his butt even though I was desperate to ram my tongue into his hairy funk hole.

Turning my attention back to his cock, I ran my tongue

over the sensitive knob before plunging my face down into his pubes.

"Holy shit, you got a velvet throat. Don't think I can take much more of it."

I wanted to prolong his enjoyment, so I turned my attention back to his balls, slobbering spit all over them, and he moved down in the chair so I had better access. That gave me better access to his ass-crack.

"Honey, why don't you take another snort or two because I'm gonna do something real special for ya. You'll love it so just relax."

He unscrewed the cap and took six large snorts before offering me the bottle. I topped up my already wild libido and waited for the buzz to kick in. He moaned. I shifted his ass for better leverage. When I judged he was at the height of his buzz I parted his cheeks, sucked his wet hole and shoved my tongue in as far as I could go. He bucked, pushing himself back on my mouth so I could suck his asshole, smearing my face in his crack to get all his scent on my lips. I sucked and chewed his cunt until he was wriggling frantically trying to get away from my grip.

"That's so fuckin' intense," he groaned, jerking his cock. I knew if I wanted to taste his spunk I'd have to relinquish my grip on his ass. Coming up for air I put my mouth over his cock, feeling the blood pumping that meant he was close to coming. I deep-throated him once more for good luck then moved my lips back up to the top half of his prick, concentrating my tongue and suction action there.

It was a matter of moments before I felt the pulse catapulting up his cock shaft to splatter in my mouth. I sucked hungrily at the knob, drawing out every spurt, storing it in my mouth to show him. When they subsided, I dragged my lips over the underside of his glans then across the crown until I'd suctioned up every bit of his juice.

I looked up at the ex-con, opening my mouth, sticky mucous stringing between my lips as the spunk puddled at the back of my throat, my tongue dripping spooge.

"Swallow it, bitch. Show me how much you fuckin' love it."

I tasted the salty slime on my tongue then gulped it down like a giant mucous oyster slithering into my stomach.

"That's a good bitch," he smiled, thumbing my mouth open to make sure it was all down my gullet. I noticed his cock was still semihard so I hoped I still had a chance at getting him in my ass. There wouldn't be much foreplay but that was okay, all I wanted was slam-bam-no-thanks-necessary-ma'am.

I grabbed the lube bottle, squished lube onto my fingers and then lay back on the bed, lifting my legs so I could finger my hole, showing him how eager I was.

"You like my cunt, baby? Look how I like to feel my fingers inside. I wish it was a big man's cock."

He didn't bite, just sat there absentmindedly playing with himself. I lubed my hole good, pulling the lips apart to get at the muscle inside. I ran my greasy fingers over one of my favorite dildos then, taking a quick hit of poppers, I placed the rubber cock against my ass entrance—and pushed. I gritted my teeth against the pain but felt my sphincter spread wide open to take the rubber intruder. I rested for a moment to get used to the pain. I was flying. Sure a rubber substitute is better than nothing when the real thing's not available, but there was a perfectly good cock just feet away and I wanted it in my ass.

"Stroke that big hot cock, baby. Get it hard. Get it real hard. Imagine it's in my pussy, in my ass cunt. You feel so good inside me, honey. Going deep, fucking me rough like a real man does.

Feel me gripping your shaft as you ram it in, filling me with your fuck seed."

I saw his eyes glaze over and his hand speed up.

"You like my pussy, honey? Yeah, hot pussy for your cock. Come on and fuck me, honey. Fuck me hard. You want my cunt, honey. Fill it with your huge fuckin' cock. I bet it won't even fit in my little hole, but you'll force it in. Rape my hole. Come on fucker, shove it in my cunt."

He stood up and kneeled on the bed behind me, yanking out the dildo, grabbing my waist, hoisting me over so my face was in the pillow. Without warning, his prick invaded my guts, plugging my hole totally. He didn't stop pushing until his stomach hit my ass. I was pinned to the bed, unable to move except to push back against him.

"Holy fuck, you're tight. Hottest ass cunt I ever had."

I flexed my sphincter as he battered my hole, keeping up a barrage of cheap whore porn talk, which he matched expletive for expletive. I couldn't have wished for a rougher lover. There was no finesse to his fucking, no consideration for me; his entire concentration was in his cock and getting off regardless of who or what was his partner. He was a sex animal and I loved it. I wanted it rough, and that's how he was doing me. Downside: he wouldn't last long. Neither did I.

I felt his smaller load of hot spunk shoot inside my ass as I blew a stream of my own all over the blanket on my bed. He pulled out, sticky come leaking down the back of my leg, and slapped my ass.

"Thanks, I needed that."

Without so much as a kiss or postprandial cigarette, he got under the blankets and was asleep before I'd even tidied up. I took the time to empty my student cards and my sole credit card from my wallet, leaving enough of my hard-earned cash that he wouldn't bother looking for any more, before placing the wallet carefully on the table. It pays to be careful.

I wiped my ass but kept it lubricated before getting into bed, keeping far enough away from him that any sudden movement in my sleep and I'd be on the floor. My precautions were well justified, because in the early hours of the morning I was awakened by the blunt head of his very hard cock pushing for entrance to my ass. I shifted enough to give him easy admission and he pounded into me as he held my throat. He didn't last long, shooting his load then rolling off me and going back to sleep.

In the morning when I woke up, he was gone. So was my wallet.

I never bothered securing the window again, hoping, I suppose, for a return visit. But in the three years I lived there, it never happened again.

DADDY MACK

R. Talent

Cleveland, Ohio, 1991

D amn, baby boy," the husky voice of the hairy, slim and
sweaty forty-nine-year-old black man clamping down
on my ankles groaned, "You got some of that good asshole,
don'tcha boy?"

The problem with growing up a noticeably handsome nine-
teen-year-old of both African American and Mexican descent in
the slums of Cleveland, Ohio is that if every other word coming
out of your mouth isn't talking about breaking in some pussy or
making some bread to get some pussy, then you had a tendency
to stick out like a sore thumb from the rest of your crew.

It wasn't like I was a virgin or anything. It was just that
pussy didn't do anything for me. In fact, I knew that long before
I started getting some. But in my attempt to fit in, I continued to
do the deed with the girls, hoping that one day I could muster
up the same enthusiasm about ho-hopping as most of my boys

did. So I was a far cry from Daddy Mack, this old head who came around the way talking about "squeezing" in between a long silky pair of legs as if he was bragging about his bravado role in a famous spectator sport.

It could be argued that I was only nineteen. Grown enough that I could've easily bounced elsewhere to avoid these useless conversations, but the only reason I stuck so close to my crew was because I knew Daddy Mack was going to eventually pop up. The funny thing was, even though I knew I had a hard-on for guys, I wasn't even looking at Daddy Mack like that. Sure he was cute, in a mature sort of way, standing about five-foot-nine with milky skin that wouldn't brown no matter how long he sat out in the blistering sun. I might have thought he was handsome if it wasn't so well hidden behind the flashiness of his latest threads or the chunky gold chains or the diamond studs in his ear or the sparkly rings that adorned every one of his long skinny fingers.

But no, I had my eyes locked on this guy in my HVAC class named Chachi, a short thickset Trinidadian dude with this incredibly powerful he-man build. He looked like he was dipped in a chocolate-chip-brown finish that made me fiendish for a bite of cookie every time I saw him. Chachi was much closer to my age and had this bad-boy swagger, riding in on his Suzuki motorcycle, fresh out of prison and trying to get his life back on track. He was ahead of his time, showing no shame in flirting with me out in the open like it was nothing. Even in front of potential booty calls that thought his authoritative accent was incredibly sexy or in front of instructors that told him to cool it. It didn't matter. Like I said, he wasn't bashful in letting every-body know that he liked what he saw. Of course, being a young man asserting my manhood, I was slightly embarrassed and angry, putting him in check. And yet secretly I was turned on like an inferno that needed desperately to be cooled off.

Then one day as I made my way over to the bathroom to take a piss, and as I was getting ready to walk out, I was talked back over to the sink. I don't know how his little ass did it, but he had me posted up against the countertop with his hands roaming against my ass, kissing me like I had never been kissed before. When I wasn't in euphoria already, I felt his cumbersome friend hurting to come through his pants. I won't even lie. I was hot in the ass, even though I never had a dick a day before in my life. I got so soaking wet at the possibility, it wasn't even funny. It didn't go any farther than that, though, and within the next couple of days I was walking around feeling like something was missing from my asshole.

I probably should've known that Chachi was simply going for a fuck with the pretty redbone he thought he flipped, but I had already made plans for him to be my boyfriend on the simple basis that he was a man about his interest in me. And in my horny naivete, I thought I would make it official with sex. The problem was we were both living at home with our families and so broke that scoring a room at the roach motel was too rich for our blood. So I took my cue from him and lured him into one of the bathroom stalls and offered up the best blow job an enthusiastic first timer could ever deliver. I bobbed and weaved, sucked and licked, and was rewarded with a mouthful of man-milk that I drank proudly because I thought Chachi was my man.

The day after, as I was expecting life to be lovey-dovey with my new man, he delivered one of the coldest pimps I ever heard, appreciating me for putting him on, but explaining he wasn't in the business of fucking around with a knob-slobber out of the stalls.

I was devastated. I was so devastated that instead of catching the bus home, I walked five miles in the drizzling rain just to get there. And when I got there, I found out that I had lost my house key, leaving me to scour the neighborhood hoping to find one of my homeboys at home. I was batting a thousand before this Cadillac pulled up beside me.

"What it is, playa?" Daddy Mack shouted from his car with the mobile phone inside.

"Nothing," I said somberly, keeping my focus on the sidewalk straight ahead.

"I would ask if you need a lift, but you're already at home. So the only reason a man would fuck around with this pneumonia is if he really got to get somewhere or he lost his mind over a piece of tail."

"I just passed up two bus stops." I mouthed, as he slow-strolled next to me in his ride.

"There's always other fishies in the sea," Daddy Mack comforted, as I was noticing the graying strain around his temples. "As good-looking as you are, you won't have a problem getting another scallywag on your jock."

"It ain't even like that. It's just been a bad day all the way around. To top it off I'm locked out of the house and can't find anywhere to go."

"Hop on in then, my brotha. You can hang out at the crib with me for a while."

About five minutes later, we were inside his two-bedroom house down the street. Although, we had known each other since forever, we didn't have the kind of relationship where he invited me over to his house. So I was sort of set back that the décor of the place reminded me of my uncle's old bachelor pad back in the '70s with the black-light artwork of naked black women with Afros. The slight difference was that part of the room did have more of a trendier flow of the time period with neon innuendoes.

We sat on his soft leather sofa, and he offered me a cold drink. I accepted, being the only two choices he had were water and beer. I wasn't thirsty. I was just desperate to prove my manhood again by gulping down a couple of bottles of the awful-tasting brew.

"What's wrong?" Daddy Mack asked after he popped opened his third bottle.

"No offense, man. I appreciate everything you've done for me, but I really don't feel like talking about it. It's just as sad as it is embarrassing."

"What? Having performance issues already, Youngblood?" Daddy Mack asked seriously.

"Naw," I laughed, thinking about the job I did on Chachi less than twenty-four hours ago, sipping on my second brew, "nothing like that."

"Okay, then," Daddy Mack conceded. "If you don't feel like getting into it with me, that's fine. I understand. I've been there. But whatever you do, Youngblood, don't let that shit build up in your heart over a piece of ass. You hear?"

I nodded in agreement.

We engaged in a bit of small talk on some other subjects between sips, with the most astonishing revelation to come out being that he wanted to get me "alone" for a "very long time," to break me free from some of those "lames" that I hung out with. He told me that I had a good head on my shoulders with school and stuff. I would've left his words at face value if it wasn't for Chachi teaching me a few things before he kicked me to the curb.

He started coming at me with that game, too. Wanting to get me alone to talk and stuff. The only difference was that Chachi was a lot more blunt about why he wanted to get me alone, as opposed to Daddy Mack claiming that he wanted to swim inside of my head.

Then, too, I knew that I could've simply been overthinking my step.

Daddy Mack was a playa. He had that charisma that made it seem like he thought you were the only person in the room when he was holding court in a crowd full of people. He had that thing that if you weren't around him, there was something big you were missing out on.

He was just wrapping up another one of his infamous sex stories when he asked if it was cool for him to turn on the TV. I had no objections. He went for the remote to turn it on, and up popped this woman getting hit in the eye by a jet of yellowish cum.

"Oh, damn! I'm sorry. I get off on this freaky shit. It always gives a brotha some fresh ideas on how to put it on that stankin' pussy."

"Yeah, without a doubt," I said grinning, looking at this humungous dick on the man on television.

The only time I got to watch stuff like that was at the handful of bachelor parties I was fortunate enough to go to, or whenever I felt like hauling my ass over to one of those jack-off theaters whenever I felt the pressure build up.

"You want to keep it here or something a little bit more PG-thirteen?"

"This is cool, right here," I said making a failed attempt not to sound too eager.

We sat around watching for a few minutes more and perhaps in the second scene was this blonde-headed white girl getting eaten out by this beefy black dude. It was nothing new, just the foreplay needed to get to the action. But this guy just kept at it like she was his last supper until it became clear that he was going to tongue-torture her to pleasure forever.

Out of nowhere, Daddy Mack, with his hand in his lap, looked me dead in the eye and asked, "Not in a queer way, but I always wonder how a dude would feel if he got ate out that way?"

"I wouldn't know. I'd think it probably felt the same way as getting your dick sucked with the nerve endings and such," I said, repeating something I had heard.

"I thought so, too. When I was stationed over in Germany, I had this buddy who said that he got off on his wife eating him out. He said it was better than getting sucked off. I told him that I would have to take his word for it because my asshole was a one-way street!"

"Yeah, I know that's right!" I laughed nervously, though in the back of my mind I was sure it was one of the weirdest things a man could say to another man after watching something like this.

The more we watched the screen, the more I thought about it; in hindsight, I could see that Daddy Mack was baiting me all along, always using me as a physical example in most of his stories. Touching me here and touching me there. Even though I wasn't into him like that, I always managed to get the best view of his big-ass dick running down his leg behind his thin hand. It definitely caught my attention in the tight pants he wore. And not like I wanted to cop a feel or something as much as I was thinking why couldn't I be packing like that? Don't get me wrong. I was always proud of the size of my dick. It was just the idea of bulging out of my pants that always intrigued me.

"Damn, he's eating that pussy up!" Daddy Mack proclaimed after a few more minutes. "The way this is running I'll probably score some more tail before he scores once!"

I laughed.

"Shit," Daddy Mack continued, "I can probably drop you off on the block, pick up a chick from around the way, fuck her and feed her and he still wouldn't be finished with his meal."

"I don't have any doubts about that."

"As awful as this may sound, my last fuck didn't last this long."

"Damn. When was that?"

"If you leave it at just a mic job, then it would've been this morning. About a couple of days ago, if you're talking about giving that middle eye a black eye. So what about you, Mr. Lovah?"

"It's been a minute," I said slowly.

"That's all right, nothing to be ashamed of. Keep that mind on your education, make that paper, and soon there will be so much pussy coming at you that you'll probably have to throw some of it back."

"I hope not."

"I hope not either," Daddy Mack winked.

We watched a few minutes more with nothing much changing with the action, except that the woman was about to pass out from the pleasure, begging for some dick. I knew I was hard, but I hadn't realized just how hard Daddy Mack was until I saw it tower out of his naked lap like some veiny lighthouse.

"Whoa!" I said trying my best not to look directly at it.

I knew he was long through his pants print, about nine and a half to ten inches or so. But I didn't know that his pound-cake-colored dick was so damn thick, too. Just like a plantain.

"Sorry, man. I forgot all about you, you being so quiet over there and all. My mind was somewhere else. Like I said before, I get off on this freaky shit."

I just looked over at him a bit shaken up. He didn't say it as if he was implying something. It just felt like he was as uncomfortable as I was.

"It's cool," I said, comforting him.

"Might as well get comfortable you...because I ain't going

anywhere until I get it out and I can go the distance when I want to."

I nervously undid my belt and my pants and let my leaky-tipped dick spring out. As I kept my pants on over my ass, he slid his down to his ankles reminding me that he lived alone and that he had some leather cleaner in the back just in case I started to sweat. Even so, I kept my pants up.

"Like I was saying, I was just thinking that I wouldn't mind munching on some ass, and then poke him for not poking her already."

"No disrespect, man, but that sound like a fairy move," I said, keeping my eyes glued straight to the screen.

"It'd only be some fairy shit if you weren't secure in your manhood in the first place."

"Maybe you're right, folk."

"I know I am. Let's say we're behind bars and I say that I got your back if you give me some head. What would you say?"

"Hell, naw, folk," I said seriously guilty.

"We're in prison. There isn't anything else your pretty ass can do other than get took. It doesn't mean that you're going to spend the rest of your life on your knees sucking dick. You're just doing what needs to be done in order to survive."

"Why are we even going there? Neither one of us is in prison."

"You're absolutely right," Daddy Mack conceded softly. "I'm just looking around the room and seeing two grown-ass men with their dicks out. One of which is getting a case of mad munchies and another that has the ability to tell me if my German bud was right."

I looked over at the screen where echoes of pleasure were being emitted, and I thought about that day I felt like something was missing out of my asshole.

"I can't even lie. That sounds like something I could get into," I said sliding my pants off of my ass and looking over at him.

"How would you know if you never tried it?"

"I won't tell if you don't," I joked.

"You better not tell! I got a rep to protect. And if you flap your gums, then I'm going to have to beat your ass." Daddy Mack laughed with a rope of seriousness in his husky tone.

"You have to tongue it first," I said, letting my words linger in the air for about a minute, and then pulling my baggy jeans over my big boots. "So if I let you do it you promise not to tell anybody?"

"Just between you and me, kid," Daddy Mack said, grinning and leaning over on top of me.

It took us a few seconds to find the right position, but after we got it together I was lying naked on the sofa with one leg on the ground and the other draped over the back. Daddy Mack just dove in with his tongue, bringing my ass up to his face and teasingly licking the outside of my hole. I didn't know what to expect from this unusual experience, as it was more weird than pleasurable, because of my erratic uneasiness with the biggest player in the neighborhood making me his latest conquest. I felt his finger reach behind my leg and pinch my nipples in this peculiar way; my butthole flared open and my dick strained just a bit harder. I didn't know what to do. I was so lost in this flooding pleasure that I just pushed his face to get his tongue farther in there. He seemed to expect this, swabbing the inner circle of my hole and then occasionally sticking his wet tongue so far in there that I was hungry for more.

"Oh, goddamn," I cried.

It was the first time I had felt something like this, and I was fighting harder than ever to keep my manhood in check. But it didn't do no good. I was rolling my phat booty all over his face

and trying my best to stay tight-lipped about wanting his dick
up in me, since I had never been fucked and it was barely a day
before I had thought Chachi was going to be my first.

"You gonna let me melt up in this bitch, Youngblood?"
Daddy Mack said, pulling his face away from my tender hole.

"Huh?" I huffed, catching my breath.

"Let me stick my man up in that sweet spot! Have you singing
real pretty for me."

"No, man," I said, quivering, him replacing his tongue with
one thin stabbing finger that was just sinking into me with very
little resistance.

"Huh?"

"No," I whimpered, another finger barreling its way into me.

"Yeah, you are. Can't you hear it? Can't you feel it? It's got
Daddy Mack's name written all over it. Let Daddy Mack show
you that there's nothing for a sweet redbone thing like you to
be scared of."

I wasn't aware how light-headed I was until he pulled me
straight over his lap, where I felt his dick and the thick slimy goo
it was covered in against my pubes. Before I could get myself
ready, he bounced me up on his lap and the next thing I knew I
felt this incredible pain shooting up the center of my ass.

"Shhh!" he hissed at my bawling on top of him. "Give it a
minute. I'll make you feel real good, I promise."

I was so sure I had pulled something, it didn't occur to me
that with him eating me like he had and the slippery stuff on his
dick, the entry had been made easier.

My eyes were screwed tight and I was still gritting my teeth
hoping that he might be right about eventually making me feel
good. And he was. The pain subsided, but it didn't become the
flood of pleasure either. I was sort of stuck in this middle ground
that was turned into something more when he started sucking

on my nipples. The sensation charged straight through my dick
and my hole again, and I instantaneously bucked against him a
couple of times. He returned the favor and bucked twice more,
thinking that I was getting into it.

"I told you. That Daddy Mack feels good up inside of you,
don't it?"

I was still breathless and confused and inexperienced and
nervous about getting into it, and it didn't help me get any more
perspective when I felt the sting of his rough hands slapping my
ass as he bounced me up and down on his lap.

"Now you know why those bitches love me so, right?" He
laughed against my incoherent grumblings.

I was still in this confused state about fifteen minutes into
our fucking when he laid me down on the shag rug next to
the glass coffee table. I don't know what it was then; maybe it
could have been him being on top of me or having more room
to maneuver, but when he pinned my legs back and guided his
thick dick into me he instantly became part owner of my hole.
He started out rolling on top of me, taking these forceful lunges
into me before he pulled back, grabbing my ankles and taking
these insanely long and deep strokes that made me sign my
entire butthole over to him.

"Whoa-whee! This shit is better than pussy!" Daddy Mack
bragged, pouring with sweat between my legs.

He went in for another round of rabbit-fucking before he just
pulled on out.

I thought he was getting ready to bust a nut somewhere on
my body. But he didn't even grab his greased dick, staring down
at me proudly.

"What?" I asked, while he just looked down at me with his
hand on his waist, panting and sweating.

He let out a laugh. I got the joke when I felt that my legs were too stiff to bring back down.

"Reach on back there," he ordered. "Before you couldn't get the head of a bobby pin back there, and now you can dig yourself out with four fingers!"

He was right. I rubbed my fingers back there and all four slid in like it was nothing. I was more than a little freaked out, not knowing if it was permanent or not. And before I could share my concerns, he moved my fingers out of his way and ploughed his way back into me.

"That's what I'm talking about. Let me hear that asshole talk." Daddy Mack groaned as he fucked me with a new sense of urgency.

I thought I had taken all that I could when I felt his low-hanging balls beat loudly against my hole. But that was nothing compared to the wobbly sound coming out of my asshole every time he dove in. It was almost like I was farting through thin plastic without the gas or the muscle control back there.

"I'm about to put all these babies in your belly, you hear?" he warned gently, contrary to his otherwise diligent fucking.

Daddy Mack grunted, pounding me harder and faster, making sure I felt every stroke. And even though he had worked me loose long before then, somehow or another, my hole quickly tightened up around his swollen dick just as it pulsed around my wet wall ready to spew junk.

"Oh, goddamn, motherfucker!" Daddy Mack barked.

His gnarled face twitched something monstrous as this warm sensation spread within my well-used hole and throughout my intestines.

Daddy Mack collapsed on top of me, kissing me on my neck erratically along with kicking out the rest of his lingering load with these sporadic thrusts back into my hole before he stopped.

He lay on me for about ten minutes. I thought he was half asleep, but then he found this new burst of energy to lift himself up off of me. He immediately told me to put on my clothes. I didn't know what to say or think as I did so, looking for him to say something, but he never did. He just opened up the front door for me to walk out, quietly told me to get into his Cadillac and drove me back over to my house. I tried thanking him for the life as I got out of his car, but the only thing he did was grunt.

I went about my way. He went about his.

I was so put off with Daddy Mack and Chachi that I did my best in trying to avoid them. It worked well for a while. The more I saw them the angrier I got. The way I had let them use me and throw me away like that. I hated both of them every time I jacked off, thinking about them inside of me like that.

Upon graduation from vocational school, I turned my back on Cleveland just like Daddy Mack and Chachi did me and moved on down to Cincinnati.

WHEN MARRIED
MEN COME
IN CARS

Jeff Funk

Even though he's straight, Joe once showed me his dick on a dare. I'd been chatting him up hard-core, telling him that gay men give dudes the *best* blow jobs, and that if he ever needed my services, I would hand him a girlie magazine and he could spread his legs and enjoy. Each time I mentioned this—and it was often—his eyes would get a far-off look. "I've heard that you fellas give good head," he'd say.

He always wore the same ratty faded blue jeans, until finally, the crotch busted through, yet he continued to reach for them. It was as if they were his standard uniform. He walked his dog first thing in the morning with those drafty blue jeans, and said his morning wood sometimes poked through.

"Shit, I dare you to poke it out the hole and let it flop out the crotch," I said one day when he was wearing them.

He did it.

Oh, yes. When I got my first glimpse of Joe's bold beauty, I decided that I needed to seduce him into letting me taste it.

We worked the second shift together at the bread factory near the St. Mary's River. Joe was at ease around gay guys. None of the other straight factory workers were secure enough to not only be friends with an openly gay guy, but to joke around sexually, too.

The men gave Joe a lot of shit for hanging with the queer, but he told 'em all to fuck off, which made me admire him all the more—as if I weren't already having a major crush on this straight stud. It was a dance of sexual male bonding, toeing at forbidden lines in the form of dark humor. Joe got it; he was down.

There were rumors that I sucked him off during our half-hour lunch and for each fifteen-minute break. But no, man. We were busy getting a buzz and talking about sex.

Straight men are exotic to me. Hell, I can get a gay guy anytime. My friend William often said, "It's like shootin' fish in a barrel to get a gay guy." He goes for the so-called straight boys, too. The "big-game hunters" among the tribe go after the ultimate prize: *heterosexual men.*

And I knew Joe's wife didn't give good head. He told me she said it made her gag. She only *licked* his dick—no insertion into her friggin' mouth, which could actually use something in it more often to plug the hole. Yappy airhead.

A man needs blow jobs; they're the spice of life.

Poor Joe.

If he wanted warm mucous membrane and true wetness caressing his cock, he had to stick it in her. Said she squeals and giggles the whole damn time he's doing her and this pisses him off.

As we sat on the roof of the bread factory tonight during our nine o'clock fifteen-minute break, he told me this pitiful tale once again and was more steamed about it than usual. He looked at me with true disgust. "It's like she's laughing at me that she doesn't give head—nope, just lies there acting like we're doing something *funny*. That's when I plow her pussy—*hard*. Punishment. You know?" He shrugged his shoulders as if to say, *What are ya gonna do?* He was reassuring himself. He looked like a man who was blow-job deprived. It showed.

"I don't know, man," I said with soft comfort to my tone. *Maybe he didn't feel desired*, I pondered. "Women are weird. Glad they're in *your* area of the dating pool." I filled my lungs with hot smoke from my one-hitter and passed it to him. "I like easy dick."

"Yeah?" He flicked a black mini-Bic lighter, cupping one hand around it to keep the wind from snuffing out the flame, and took a long pull of his own. On the exhale, he coughed out, "Damn you must get blow jobs *all the time*, huh?"

My hearing went wonky then: the traffic on Sallee Street sounded like ocean waves to me, and Joe's words sounded deeper than his normal bass timbre. "Couple times a week or so," I said. "The thing about getting random head is you have to be willing to *give* as well. That's Good Dick Karma." I nodded slowly, glancing at his crotch once.

Joe got that far-off look and smiled in such a way that his whiskered dimples showed. It was as if his dick woke up and enjoyed the sound of that—*blow jobs?*—and I thought to myself, *This stallion turns hyper-dirty when I get him high.* "Do you want to go for a drink tonight after we get off?" Joe asked. The allure of his glassy doe eyes pulled at me when I saw that they were tinted with that horny squint of his. The man was feeling rascally.

"Sounds good, man. So...you pound a pussy *good*—sounds like. Jeez. That's badass, ya stud," I said and then play-punched his arm, which got a grin out of him.

As steamy thoughts of him as a relentless rammer of cock took hold, I made no effort to hide the fact that I *needed* to adjust my junk. Then I watched as a night train passed behind the bread factory. The cruising queers were out, making their usual laps. Ole Kirby's rattletrap junker—one even worse than mine—had been by three times already. Most of the drivers of these cars were the cheating *curious* husbands, ministers, school administrators, counselors and all of the rest of the closeted men. The sneaky ones. On any given night, there's always a lot of straight dick out there for the sucking—a *lot* of dick.

I nodded out of my trance, which had begun to feel as if disco music were underscoring my thoughts with a beat so intense that I could feel it through my shoulders and hips. I said, "Beer and a buzz. That's a plan."

The hour and forty-five minutes went fast till the end-of-shift whistle sounded. Guys took off their plastic gloves and their uncomfortable sanitation hats. The bread line had halted on the various levels throughout the cavernous building.

At the lockers, I said, "Let's take my car."

"Shotgun!" Joe shouted.

"Dude, you're the only one goin' with."

"Shotgun!" he repeated and then ran out the door to my LeSabre.

I shook my head and followed him into the muggy night air. I felt something different, a fluttering in my belly. In fact, I trembled. I knew that there was a sexual charge building in both of us, one that needed a release.

Due to a minor incident with a guardrail, the passenger side of my junker was banged up badly and held together with black duct tape. The door only opened halfway, but Joe's athletic agility allowed him to slip in and fall onto the wide seat fine. However, we both heard the sound of metal creaking and a spring broke. Abruptly, Joe's rump lowered about an inch. "When did you say you're getting that new car?"

"Oh, maybe when I've gotten my good out of *this* one? Watch your fingers," I said and then I closed the door for him in an act of chivalry.

The car started on the first try for once with only a few puffs of black smoke blasting out the back. The vehicle's motor operated in such a way that a *major* vibration shook the hell out of us. Felt good to my nuts, but then I'm kinky like that. I've got big ole bull balls and I *have* to spread my legs wide. Some men are packing olives at best, not the plums I transport with every step.

We sparked one up and then passed it to each other with our well-practiced rhythm of graceful exchange. It was only a short few blocks to the Duck In Irish Pub & Eatery. On the way, though, when we were stuck at the light on Ewing and Main, several older male cruisers drove past snail-slow. I shook my head at all of them so they wouldn't waste their time or gas. I had no intention of fucking their high-mileage sloppy asses. Besides, I had my prey sitting next to me.

It was about ten minutes past eleven when we entered the pub. They had Guinness and Killian's on tap. *Fuck yeah*, I thought. I often started with a pint or two of Guinness—at four bucks—then switched to two-dollar pints of Killian's. The smoking patio was full of hippie folk. Queer-friendly, mellow fellow *brothers*. Music lovers, artists—my type of people.

Joe fit in because he was so mellow. He was one of the rare beauties who hardly seemed to be aware of his good looks, an appealing quality that added to his allure. At six foot four and not an inch of fatty flesh on his taut torso, he was lean like a stallion, with dark hair. His thick Vandyke-style goatee had '70s porno bushiness to its mustache, which always drew my attention to his thick, full red lips. The dark whiskers encircling his mouth made his teeth look particularly white. He had a beautiful smile. I often watched his mouth when he spoke; savoring each time I saw a slip of his clean pink tongue. Secretly, I longed to kiss him and feed him my sizable serving of cock.

I thought, *I'll take him in hand and lead the way through his first walk into the land of forbidden seduction. Unless the reason he's cool with gay guys is because he's found our network of secret oral service. Maybe he keeps his shit discreet. Men are crafty at getting into trouble. They want their dicks wet. They close their eyes, think of tits—a few too many beers and suddenly: "How the hell did my dick get in my buddy's mouth?" The drunk defense. Yeah, whatever you need to tell yourself. All gay men are onto the ways of stray straight fellas, and we're forever on the prowl, searching eyes in a crowd for our next willing customer.*

Joe ordered a whiskey with cola and ice, while I stuck with a pint of frothy dark Guinness from the tap. Then we headed into the cavernous dance room and went back to a dark booth back in the farthest corner from the bar.

"Ryan, I've got something you're going to want to hear," he said with his squinty eyes.

"Oh yeah?" I said. I could feel my groin begin to stir. I'd come to look forward to hearing Joe's dirty desires because I used it as my main fantasy material for masturbation.

"No one knows about this—and you *cannot* tell anyone what I'm about to tell you."

I assured him, "Dude. I wouldn't say anything. You have my *word*. Why do you think I'm able to get guys to tell me their dirty secrets? I keep quiet, trust me."

He took another drink, and then his words were fast as if he needed to belch it out and not care that it didn't sound pretty.

"Tuesday night, Troy and I went to Copper's and there was a fuckin' *hot* chick there. Red curly hair. Classy and maybe a bit...predatory? She wanted sex."

"Yeah?"

"She was so horny, she wanted both of us."

"*Holy shit*! A threesome?"

"Honestly, she was more into my buddy," he admitted. "Troy talked her into letting me join the party. So we went to her place up by Auburn Hills. Nice pad. And once inside, we just stripped and—*fucked*."

I let out a low whistle to show my awe of his story.

"Since she liked Troy better, she wanted to kiss him. Fine by me, I thought 'cause while he had his cock filling her pussy, I used spit at first and then lube to finger her pucker, and then I slowly inched my boner inside."

"Did you wear a condom?" I asked.

"Well, yeah...to start off, I wore it. Then I figured it was just her ass and my *swimmers* wouldn't do nothin' to that. So I got rid of it. Dropped it in front of me and the damn thing stuck to my foot."

"How did it feel?"

"The slimy rubber or her asshole?"

"The hole."

"Tight." Joe suddenly stretched out his arm and waved. I turned and saw that it was Bill, the bar-back we both smoked with, who sped through while clearing tables. Joe got back to his confession. "Her hole felt like it *hugged* my cock. Felt so much better than..." his voice trailed off while he stared into space in search of lost details from the encounter, maybe mixed with guilt from the infidelity.

"Could you tell that Troy's cock was moving inside her with yours?"

"Yeah, we timed our thrusting and varied it. Tried a *bunch* of positions. This babe knew how to *fuck*, like she'd done three-somes before and liked the danger. I let Troy tongue-kiss her and play with her hair, meanwhile I would be doing a reach around to grab her tits, say, or taking advantage of her sweet ass. To answer your question, though: yes, I felt his dick inside her. His is bigger than mine," he added with a thin smile because he knew how much it would titillate me since I'd already seen Joe's meaty member. "It was like me and my buddy was *rubbing* cocks together, only we were doing it from inside her pink pussy and my boner probing that *fine* ass."

"When you felt Troy's erection pressing against yours, how did that feel?"

"Good," he said and took a large swig of his drink. I noticed the flexor muscles of his forearms ripple like a shimmer through a thoroughbred horse's powerful leg. When Joe looked at me, his steamy squint was back, only now he looked at my lips as if assessing how they might feel for sexual service.

"Did you guys grab each other?"

"By the waist, yeah. Then we grabbed each other's ass while she was sandwiched. Then we bear-hugged—so hot, all of that sticky flesh. Troy and I tried to squish as much cock inside her holes as possible. We both blew *gobs* of cum inside the redhead and then collapsed on the bed like sweaty animals. Felt fucking fantastic. Goddamn, I'm horny again thinking about it."

"Let's get out of here," I said.

He knocked back his remaining alcohol. "Let's roll bro."

We parked near the quiet loading dock of the bread factory, which was beside the railroad tracks. The St. Mary's river was a few hundred yards beyond that with thick clusters of trees lining the riverbank. It was very dark back in that corner of the company's lot and the delivery drivers wouldn't be active until third shift finished up at seven o'clock in the morning. I put the car in park and killed the engine.

"I've never done this before," Joe said.

"Relax. That seat reclines, by the way." He found the lever and leaned back and got comfortable, unzipping his pants and pulling out his dick. I turned the car key backward so we could listen to modern rock from the radio, our lullaby of lust to set the mood. "Now close your eyes," I said. "Lie back and be my toy, a dick for me to explore."

"Make it yours," he mumbled. I grabbed the shaft at the base and gobbled his knob with my full lips. I licked his sensitive piss slit and even probed it with the tip of my tongue for pearls of precum. "Yeah...suck, suck it. Ah, fuck yeah." He blew hot breath in my face, and I smelled his whiskey and smoke.

I got off on the fact that Joe squirmed so hard from my efforts. He was goddamn dirty-talking. *Vocal*—and masculine about asking for what he wanted. There was no shame. He spoke in his usual blunt, buddy-style way of talking, the only difference being the whispered unique word cocktails including the name of the Lord alongside profane words. I took every syllable and groan as praise that I was doing a fine job by my buddy. *You're very welcome,* I thought. *Straight boys' dicks taste the best. How strange to know that he'll go home and punish his yappy wife—with my saliva still drying on his cock. How would his dick smell with pussy secretions mixed with my Guinness and pot breath?*

"Mmm," I hummed while his dick was down my throat. When I pulled my lips up and tongue-swirled the throbbing flesh, I paused to whisper, "Joe, you taste *so* good. Give me your load. Gimme it. Come in my mouth."

Rivers of sweat were dripping down my face from the heavy summer air. The temperature was warm even after midnight.

To counter the dry-mouth effects of the pot, there were several times I swiped a hand over my buzzed and balding head then slopped the moisture onto his cock so I could slurp it eagerly and slip my tongue quicker under his cockhead.

He smelled wonderful. Man-stink from a day of hard work and a ripe crotch from the summer sizzle. He was a heavy precummer and I drank like a thirsty fucker. *Yum, so good*, I kept thinking to myself.

Joe put his hand on my head and ground his hips in circles to work his cock inside my red-bearded mouth. His dick was slippery, warm and fully engorged. I loved that his porky cock got even *thicker* when he was excited. It felt wonderful giving pleasure to someone I had desired for months. *I may not get to keep him, but I'll borrow him on occasion.*

Just then, his rhythmic grunts began to build in intensity. *Joe's about to blow*, I knew. I had hold of his balls too, and they were trying to pull up close to his body, only I wouldn't let them. It was maybe a little naughty of me, but I held them where they belonged: in my hand. While he was fully in the throes of firing shot after shot of jism into my mouth from his pumping cock, the passenger seat fully broke.

"Whoa! Fuck me," Joe shouted.

I swallowed his load while my eyes were closed. "Your cum is sweet."

Slowly he moved closer to me, and when his face was more than halfway to mine, I rushed forward to meet his kiss with mine. He sucked hard on my lips and the whiskers of his bushy Vandyke and my red beard ground into each other like bristles of hairbrushes stuck together. I thought, *Men kissing men, fuck yes. I'm going to savor kissing this man.* He was tender as he stroked my face. Then his tongue probed the spit and cum-like wetness inside my mouth as if he were in search of the taste of his own seed. *Cum tongue-play,* I noted.

Since he was full-on going for it—gay sex—I felt brave enough to grab hold and *feel* the hell out of every muscle the man had. The strength of his body gave me a rush as I roved my hands over the thin fabric of his black-and-white plaid buttoned work-shirt. I had been thinking he was scrawny, but he was lean and solid. A beefcake. "Such a hot body, Joe. You're beautiful."

"So are you." He blinked those dark eyelashes at me. Sudden chill bumps capered along the flesh of my arms, stirring the follicles of my fur. The power of his tenderness surged through me with warm waves.

I swallowed again and could still taste his cum in the back of my throat. I loved knowing that I had Joe's big load down my gullet and inside my tummy. Hey, I was just helping a buddy out—in fact, I was mighty glad to be of service. I love to help a fella lose a load. Their pleasure is all *mine,* is how I see it. Tonight Joe's creamy strands shot down my esophagus to join the dark lager still swishing in my belly.

Now a wind from the direction of the St. Mary's River blew through the windows of my car. We lit up and listened to more music. He was in no rush to get home, and I welcomed spending more time in his gentle company.

"A front's going through," Joe said.

"Yep, see the leaves? Upturned and silvery. They're waiting to slurp up a good rain, dude. They're rain-hungry mother-fuckers, sort of like *me.*"

"You are seriously high, aren't you?"

I looked at the moonlight on the telephone and power lines. After a few seconds pause, coolness numbed my body. Then I oriented myself. "You know...I think we broke down into some of the good stuff the bartender shared with me at karaoke the other night."

"Ha! Well, there's feeling good—and feelin' *damn* good, right buddy?" He patted my knee and left his hand there. He had hold of my leg.

"Right, Joe," I said and let out a slow exhale.

"You made me feel good. Much appreciated." He patted me twice with those firm man-hands of his.

"Anytime, man. Hey, I mean it." I reached behind and squeezed the meat of his shoulder and kneaded it as I said, "We're buddies."

That got his whiskery grin to come out. "Sorry I broke your seat, but man—it's *time* to get a different car. Ya got your good out of this one." He slid out of my car with macho motion, gently closed the door and then bumped it shut with his ass.

"Later, *brother*!" I shouted

He tapped the hood of my junker twice, much like he'd patted my leg, and then sauntered toward the side lot, knowing damn well that I was watching his every step through my cracked windshield. He knew I liked his butt. He enjoyed showing off his fine ass and the way it moved with his long strides inside of his tattered 501s.

Tonight I'd gotten inside those pants, and I knew that Joe would be back for more good head. I didn't give a shit about the broken car seat. He couldn't help himself. If anything, I'm at fault for getting him to writhe from all of the pleasure I lavished on his cock. A broken car seat is just one of the dangers that can occur when married men come in cars.

THE LUST LURE

Garland Cheffield

Hey, man, you know where I can score some pot?"

All I could do was stare like an idiot at the very hot, very shirtless Latino. He was sitting at a table by the pool. The hot summer sun was beating down on his body. My eyes weren't even trying to be subtle as they committed every minute detail of his deliciously smooth chest to memory for future masturbation sessions. Latin men had always been my weakness.

"Sorry, man," I croaked, finally finding my voice, thankful that it didn't crack. "I'm all out."

"Damn homes. I've been cravin' pot all day." He smiled devilishly. "Sure you don't have any hidden away?"

"Nah, man. I'm all out," I repeated. "If I had any I'd still be in my apartment smokin'."

"My kinda boy," he laughed, high-fivin' me. "We should smoke out sometime."

"Definitely," I said, and smiled. *Would love to smoke your dick, too,* I thought, amazed I didn't start chuckling. "See ya around."

As I walked away it took all my strength not to look back. My dick was tingling as I thought about his smooth caramel-colored skin and dark almond-colored nipples. I wanted to run my tongue all over him, especially his tattoos. I had always had an ink fetish and one of my favorite things to do was lick and suck on a hot guy's tats.

Easy boy, I told myself, shifting uncomfortably and pulling my shirt down to hide the growing bulge in my shorts, made all the more obvious due to my going commando. *Shit gurl. Why didn't you wear any panties today?* I mentally chastised myself.

Bea Arthur naked. Bea Arthur naked. Bea Arthur naked... I chanted silently over and over, not stopping until I was flaccid.

As soon as I got back to my apartment I jerked off to the image of that hot Latino. Closing my eyes, I furiously jerked my cock. Sticking a finger inside my hole I imagined it was his fat Latin cock stretching me out.

It wasn't long before I came, moaning, all over my chest.

Grabbing a towel, I sighed. I needed to get laid bad. Lately the guys I had been hooking up with on Grindr and Adam4Adam just weren't giving me the fucks I needed. I needed a man who fucked like a real man, who would get rough with me. Abuse my hole. Screw me until I screamed. Someone like that Latino. He looked like he liked it rough; like he would use a little force to get what he wanted. My dick fluttered and a couple of drops of cum leaked out.

About a week passed before I saw the hunk again. Every time I left my apartment I kept my eyes peeled for him like a hawk searching for prey.

Maybe he doesn't live in this building, I thought. *Maybe he was just visiting a friend.*

Taking my hair out of the ponytail, I let it fall around my shoulders. I loved my long hair. My father hated it. That's one of the reasons I didn't cut it.

Stepping out of the elevator, I heard someone whistle approvingly as I walked to the front door.

Turning, I gasped. It was him. He was leaning casually against the mailboxes wearing a pair of swim trunks. Little beads of water still clung to his skin. When he saw it was me, he blushed.

"Oh, sorry," he stammered, quickly looking away. "I thought you were a chick. The hair threw me off."

"It's okay," I said, smiling, though inside I was throwing a temper tantrum. He was straight. Fuck! Why were all the hot guys either straight, with someone or psycho?

"I've seen you around a lot," he said. "Every time I see you I wanna whistle or flirt with you 'cause I forget you're a boy. Besides the hair, you walk like a girl and you've got delicate features like one."

His voice got low and I started sweating. He was a huge flirt and it was driving me crazy.

"It happens all the time," I said. "Lots of straight guys think I'm a girl because I'm so fem. But they all seem to like it. Especially the bi and curious ones," I added with a little wink.

He blushed more and shifted uncomfortably. I couldn't help but giggle.

"Look," he said. "You're cute but I'm not into dudes."

"You ever been with a guy?" I asked.

"No. I've never wanted to be with a man."

"Too bad sugar," I said leaning flirtatiously against the wall and casually running my hand over my body. "Guys can be lots of fun. And it's easier to get dick than pussy."

Raising my eyebrows coyly I walked out the door. I felt his

eyes linger on my ass and gave it a little shake. I heard him cough with embarrassment and I couldn't help but chuckle.

"Laundry. How I hate doing laundry," I sang as I sorted my clothes. "I need to find me a rich husband who will take care of me."

Throwing the last of my clothes into the laundry basket I checked myself in the full-length mirror. I never went anywhere without checking to make sure I was 100 percent fabu.

"Never know who you're gonna meet," I told my reflection as I checked myself out. "Fabulous honey," I said with a snap, satisfied with what I saw. "Fabulous."

Picking up the laundry basket I sighed. I did not look cute with that thing in my arms. I looked like a maid.

I decided to take the long way to the laundry room and go by the pool. It was a hot day and I was hoping I could find a cute top, or five, who would keep me entertained for a while.

Unfortunately the pool was empty except for one guy. The straight boy. Sighing, I rolled my eyes. Talk about cruel and unusual punishment.

He was lying on one of the lounges in a tight Speedo that shamelessly showed off his bulge. My dick stirred and grew a little. I wanted to drop the laundry basket, pull that Speedo down and show him that boys give the best head.

Taking a breath to steady myself I began the long trek across the pool area.

"'Sup homes?" he asked when he saw me.

"Laundry," I answered, not trusting myself to be alone with him. I was so horny.

"Cool. Hey, can I ask you somethin'?"

Yes, you can stick your cock in my ass and make me your cum Dumpster.

"Sure."

He flopped over onto his stomach. His Speedo rested low on his ass, giving me a peek at his crack. God, I was about to explode.

"Do you know any girls in this complex? I need some pussy bad."

"Sorry, man," I answered completely disappointed. "I don't really know any of the girls in this building well enough to set up a booty call."

"Fuck," he moaned running his hands over his face. "I'm goin' through a dry spell. I haven't gotten any pussy in a month."

I didn't know how to respond to that. All I said was, "Sorry." It just seemed the polite thing to say.

"Thanks anyway, homes. We still gotta smoke a bowl sometime."

"Sure sugar," I said walking away, shaking my ass just a little more than I needed to.

"Outrageous. My sex drive," I sang along to Britney while I threw my clothes into the washer. I always brought my iPod with me wherever I went.

It wasn't long before I really started getting into it, shaking my ass like I was in a room full of horny old men with fists full of dollar bills.

An approving whistle made me jump, dropping the clothes I was holding. Taking my headphones out I turned and couldn't believe what I saw. It was the hottie. He was leaning lazily against the doorframe. My eyes were immediately drawn to the way his bright blue Speedo hugged his dick.

"Forget that I'm a boy again?" I asked leaning against the washer.

"No. I know that little ass," he said with a small smile.

"Wh...what?"

"I need to fuck. Bad," he answered.

"So what do you want me to do about it?" I asked flirtatiously.

"Suck my dick," he said pulling his Speedo down a little bit. He had no pubes. My dick was instantly hard. I hated body hair on guys. "I know you're into me."

"Maybe I am," I answered. "But I thought you were into girls," I said casually.

"I am," he answered honestly. Locking the door, he walked over to me. "But you're fem." He fingered my long hair. "And with your hair, it'll be just like getting a blow job from a chick. Just don't talk."

"Oh," I said. "Looking for a cure for your lust sugar?"

All he did was grin.

I couldn't believe this was really happening. Had I walked onto a porn set? I couldn't help but look to see if there were cameras and a sleazy director in the room.

Leaning closer, I moved in for a kiss. Quickly he pushed me away.

"No kissing," he said firmly. "I may let you suck my dick but I'm not gay. I've never kissed a man and I never will."

"Can I kiss your chest and stomach?" I asked. I really wanted to suck on his large dark nipples and run my tongue over his pecs and stomach.

He thought about it for a few minutes, weighing the pros and cons before saying, "Sure," very slowly, drawing each letter out.

I kissed his hard pecs before flicking my tongue rapidly against his dark nipples. He shuddered as I bit and tugged on them.

He pushed me to my knees, making me moan. Licking and kissing his flat stomach I quickly pulled his Speedo down, freeing his thick uncut dick.

I gasped and licked my lips greedily. I couldn't wait to deep-throat that monster. He was so thick I could barely wrap my fist around it.

"Suck it, you little bitch," he demanded, pushing my face toward his hardness. I was over the moon. I loved when guys called me names. Bitch. Slut. Whore. Cocksucker. Fag boy. It drove me crazy.

I opened my mouth, and he pushed himself all the way in. Even though I didn't have a gag reflex I was still surprised I could take all of him. I had never deep-throated a cock as big as his.

He moved my hair so that it covered my face, creating the illusion I was a girl. My hands gripped his tight, hard ass as he slowly fucked my mouth. His salty-sweet precum trickled down my throat.

I sucked his cock with loud slurping sounds, making it glisten. He held my head tightly in place. His ass clenched and unclenched and he groaned with satisfaction.

"Oh, yeah. You do that so good, you little slut. You love my cock in your mouth, don't you? You love being my little cocksucker. Fuck. I love the feel of your lips wrapped around my dick."

All too soon he took his dick out of my mouth. Gripping my shoulders, he picked me up, turned me around, bent me over a dryer and pulled my shorts down. Slowly he ran his hand over the curve of my ass before slapping it.

Kneeling down behind me, he spread my cheeks wide and buried his face deep in my ass. My knees wobbled and I moaned as he licked my hole. From the way he was doing it I knew he was imagining it was pussy, but I didn't care. He was very skilled with his tongue. It was the rim job of my life.

My moans rose to high falsetto squeaks as he shoved his

tongue inside me and awakened every one of my G-spots. Pounding the dryer, I screamed and nearly passed out.

"Oh, shit," I moaned. "That tongue should be illegal."

He pulled his tongue out of me and slapped my ass hard.

"Thought I told you not to talk."

With one good, hard thrust he shoved his throbbing cock into my hole. My eyes bugged out and I gasped. He was so big. I loved the feel of his monster stretching out my hole.

Holding my hips in place, he fucked me like a champ. His balls slapped against me, and his dick pulsed lustfully inside me.

Pulling my hair into a ponytail, he roughly yanked my head back. I was in Heaven. I loved it when guys pulled my hair.

"I'm gonna cum," he announced breathless.

No sooner were the words out of his mouth than he shot an impressive load inside me. I squeezed my hole around his cock, milking cum out of his balls. My legs wobbled and I fell, exhausted, onto the dryer. He gave a few quick thrusts making sure every last drop ended up inside me before pulling out. He gave my ass a quick pat and pulled his Speedo back up.

"That was great," I barely breathed out.

"Yeah, it was," he agreed.

Slowly I lifted my torso off the dryer and, with shaking arms, pulled my shorts back up.

"Don't tell anyone about this," he warned, before walking out of the laundry room.

Sighing, I slumped against the machine. That was the fuck of my life. It was a dream come true. I had done what thousands of gay boys dreamed of doing: been fucked by a real-life straight boy.

HIGH IN THE
SALT WIND

Nick Arthur

It was the Fourth of July, and everybody was down at Baz's beach house. Well, Baz's parents' beach house, but since they weren't there, it was Baz's. And the rest of ours for the weekend: Kimmel, Jason, Anthony, Sam B., Sam K., Little Gary, and more. I was forgetting somebody for sure, because I was lying in the hammock and could hear the soft break of the waves over the dune behind me. It was hot today, and I took a sweaty nap on the beach while Baz and everybody else set up the keg. Now that was already kicked and Baz was shot-gunning cans of Highlife while his girlfriend filmed it for Facebook. He's already uploaded a bunch of clips: Sam B. and Sam K. lip-synching Slim Shady, Anthony popping out of the fridge with a beer when Baz opens the door, Kimmel asleep with a chub. Baz loved his Facebook videos.

The sun was just starting to set over the Bay and the Christmas lights Baz's mom has rigged up to a timer were snapping on around the shiny wooden bar and the edges of the patio.

The lights climbed the stairs to the deck, and one strand lit up the weatherworn gazebo topping the broken hot tub—Baz's sister and Kimmel fucked up the pump or something the first day we got here. Too fucking bad about that hot tub. But there weren't any other girls here anyway, and at least I found this hammock tucked down by the dune. I tipped the last of my beer to my lips and drain it as I heard Baz and Sam K. bellowing with laughter inside the house. Those two were the biggest guys here—muscles and fat—and they laughed big as if they would tilt right over.

Far down the beach a short burst of cherry bombs *ratatatated* and then a lone firework shot up bloomed in the purplish sky. As it flashed, I noticed somebody wandering down from the edge of the patio. I took out my phone but I hadn't gotten any new texts. I rested it on my belly.

"What's up, buddy," said the figure coming toward me, and I saw that it was Little Gary. He'd always been the shortest guy we knew, but stocky and solid enough so that he was way better than Baz or me when were all on the wrestling team forever ago. Little Gary, with his hard swagger and lean muscles, was the only one who lasted. He still had all that swagger but hadn't grown any taller.

He walked up to the hammock and I stretched out one foot and dropped my arm over the side to stop my gentle swing. Even though it was the start of a swallowing night sky, little Gary sported neon-orange sunglasses. His face was flushed with drink and heat, which was as much as I could see in the glow of the Christmas lights.

Little Gary reached out and steadied the hammock and for a second it felt like I was floating. In his other hand, he was holding a 40.

"Fucking sausage party," he said, swinging his leg into the

hammock. I scooted back and over toward the rope edge to make room. Little Gary settled in with a jolt and we swung violently. Before we could tip over, he stuck out his foot and slowed us to a balanced swing. His leg was crushing mine. I felt the heat of his sunburn as he leaned forward to pass me the beer.

I took a big swig. "It sure is," I said. "How come no girls came?"

"Weren't you texting one? In Sea Isle?"

I nodded yes and took another gulp of his 40 before passing it back. "Do you want to see the picture she sent me?"

"Bra?"

"Bikini top, but it's good enough." I picked up my phone from my belly and swiped it on with my thumb. I had to hunt through her last few texts before I found it. I took a look at her and passed it over to Little Gary. I had met this girl on the beach and she groped me in the water. But by then I'd realized she was just wasting my time with all these messages.

"She's okay," Little Gary said. "Makes me think about popping wood."

"Me too, man," I said. "Wish she would text back. Or drive over here."

"We could drive to her house. I can get Baz's keys easy."

"Nah. Lives with her parents or some shit," I said. Or so she said. "Gar, you can barely drive sober anyway." He flipped me off and tilted the bottle up to his lips. He smirked as he drank. He handed me the bottle and then reached into the pocket of his bathing suit to dig out his phone. He played with it for a minute and I drank some of the beer. I leaned back and the hammock rocked until it balanced it us. After a few seconds he handed me his phone. It was a blurry picture of a hot chick in turquoise panties. It was a video and I tapped the screen to play it back. She rubbed down the front of her panties and then slipped a finger underneath the edge of them. As she rubbed her slit, Little Gary's fingers joined her from outside the frame. Then the video came to an abrupt freeze, but not before a big thick dick bounced into the camera's point of view.

My face flushed hot. The panties and the fingers had chubbed me up, and I felt myself get a lot stiffer when I thought about Little Gary's big dick fucking her.

"Holy shit," I said. "Who's that?"

"Some girl from my dorm. Wet little pussy."

"Way better than my girl." I gestured at the phone resting on my belly. My dick was making a small tent poke toward my right leg.

"Let me see it again," he said, as he reached to grab my phone. His wrist brushed against the length of my cock and I took a sharp breath. I wasn't sure if he noticed or not.

He picked up my phone and looked at the girl again. "Got anything else on here like that?"

"Probably. Let me see." I reached for it and Little Gary grabbed the bottle from my hand instead and tossed my phone back at my belly. It landed on my dick with a thud.

"Never mind," he said. "I've got more."

"You better warn me if there are any more dick shots, though, bro."

"Why dude, you a fag? Get turned on by dick?" He laughed, drained the rest of the beer and threw the empty toward the dune. As we swung back from the tiny force of his throw, he reached over and squeezed my cock through my shorts. He got me right below the glans and a jolt burned through my stomach. "You got a dick shot right here, man. Want me to leave you to take care of it?" He put one foot on the ground and moved to pull himself up out of the hammock. His fat meat was slowly unfurling in his suit. I tried to say something to stop him, but it died in my throat. As I croaked, he smiled and settled back down onto the ropes.

Little Gary reached down and rubbed the length of his shaft with his thumb. Instantly I got a big tent, too, and let it grow underneath his other hand.

I was so hard and my face was so hot it took me a second to breathe. I hooked my thumb around my waistband and tried to pull it down, but the elastic caught on my tapered cockhead like a hook, and Little Gary helped me get it out. I tucked the waistband under my throbbing sac.

"You still fucking that girl in the video?" I said as he wrapped his fist around my dick. He gripped me hard and slowly tugged on me.

"Nah. She gave me head a week ago, like quick in the car." His board shorts squeezed Gary's fat dick against his thigh. Big head, just like I had seen in the video. I reached toward it and then stopped. It twitched, and I settled my hand down on it.

"Wish she was down here. Think she'd take care of both of us?" I squeezed him and felt his pulse run through the shaft.

"Maybe," said Little Gary. "But sometimes you gotta help yourself. Right?" He slid his body toward me and his sweaty sac crushed against my wrist. He smelled like suntan lotion and beer. I pumped him and he jackhammered up into my palm. Little Gary grabbed my wrist and hawked spit onto his dick-head. I slicked my palm with spit and dropped some more on his cock. Then I wet the tip of mine, where a tiny teardrop of precum lay at the end like a pearl. I went back to jerking him off hard and fast, and he fell into a rhythm on mine, tugging and squeezing. I lay my head back and the hammock began to sway. It glided back and forth in time with Little Gary's hips, a relentless piston in my fist.

The weight of my wrist lay on his balls, and I felt the way his thrusts got tighter and more urgent as I pushed. My own nuts still ached and I offered up my hips to his fist. His fist pumped in time with his hips and the hammock was swinging like the Viking ship on the pier. The wind picked up over the crash of waves. I was pinching the rim of his dickhead where I could tell he was feeling it good and he pushed and he pushed and started to shoot.

As I felt the thick wet of his cum between my fingers my own cock spasmed and gushed all over my belly, and rocking high in the salt wind, the smell of burnt-out fireworks still drifting over the dune, I came.

IT'S ALWAYS BEST TO USE YOUR HANDS

Nick Marenco

She had discovered the Mexicans in the Ralph's parking lot down the street. The passenger seat of Rose's vintage teal 1970 Volkswagen 1600 was occupied by a brown paper bag filled with a twelve-pack of Budweiser, a carton of Newman's Own Pink Lemonade, some generic fruit Popsicles, plastic cups and a bag of ice. The backseat was packed with laundry, bedding and other odds and ends stuff she could fit. She asked four of the nine day-laborers that were leaning on a truck-sized Dumpster to follow her as she drove the three and a half blocks to the apartment.

Rose and Guy weren't venturing across America to North Carolina nor had they any desire to check out the carnivores of the green swamp preserve, but this was the U-Haul they got for their $29.95 plus 79 cents per mile. They were just relocating from Hollywood to Pasadena, so the move wasn't expected to be all that taxing. Guy was sitting on the stoop of the apartment complex they once called home, smoking a cigarette. Next to him was a cooler, some crumpled beer cans, and an empty fishbowl that didn't make the cut. Rose was standing a few feet in front of him, arms crossed. She held a half-empty cherry-colored Dixie cup of lemonade and focused on the image of a neon-green Venus flytrap that covered one side of the truck.

"They're almost done." Rose turned to look at Guy. She mindlessly tugged on the bottom button of her pink cashmere sweater with one hand, only causing it to get looser. She took a sip of lemonade and returned her attention to the flesh-eating plant that seemed to be looking back at her.

"I don't know why you hired these guys. We could've done this ourselves." Guy took a drag of his cigarette, squeezed the butt with his thumb and forefinger and stared at it as if it were a bug.

"That bed is pretty heavy. It's my great-*great* grandmother's and the dresser—"

"Yeah, I know. Forget I asked." Guy sighed.

"Besides, that slip you had in the kitchen. Can't be too careful." Rose turned and brushed the five-day-old five o'clock shadow on Guy's cheek. He pulled back, taking another drag.

"Yeah, the *slip*." Guy picked at the scabs on his exposed knees and dropped the remainder of his cigarette into an empty Budweiser can. He reached into the cooler and cracked open another. "I just can't wait for this to be over."

"Why the sour face, baby? This move was your idea. Besides, the new place is so much nicer and I have so many ideas!"

"I just hate the whole process. Moving, you know?" Guy killed off half the beer in one gulp.

"It'll be done soon. These guys are moving pretty fast." Rose plopped herself onto Guy's lap, setting her lemonade on the cooler. She dangled her arms over his shoulders and slipped her fingers through his hair that was slopped with sweat. "Why not

when we get to the new place I'll order some takeout, you take
a bath and I'll set up the television. We can have dinner on the
floor in our underwear or none at all." She smirked and looked
back at the truck then into Guys glazed over eyes. "You know,
like old times?"

"Like old times?" Guy playfully snarled at her and nibbled at
her shoulder. She giggled and batted him away.

"Not like that! You know what I mean," she teased, and
then got up to see how much more work the Mexicans had left
to do. "Well, maybe if you're good!" Rose pulled down on the
back of her jeans giving Guy a modest look at the small of her
back. She wasn't wearing any underwear. This made him grin.
He chugged down more beer.

"If I'm good?" Guy reached for the back loop of her jeans
but she jumped away, snatching up her lemonade and taking a
sip before blowing a kiss his way. He gobbled it up and swallowed it hard. "You'd only be so lucky!"

It took all four of the men to move the dresser. They were
your typical day-worker types. Not much English, skin of
varying degrees of rosy browns, short and stocky. All of them.
The one that stood outside just below the stoop motioning with
his hands was a little more fit.

He surely takes in some soccer with his amigos *in Elysian
Park on the weekends*, Guy thought. It was like he was guiding
a large aircraft for landing the way he was motioning with his
brawny arms. It seemed he was looking to Guy for his consent.
Guy just nodded at the *Latino* and pulled another Lucky Strike
from the flattened box that was sticking to his thigh from the
inside of his khaki shorts. Guy couldn't fathom what these guys
were saying but they were efficient and fast and like a good
employee the leader of the pack continued to look at him for
approval. Rose had hired them, but Guy was the man of the

house after all. This Mexican's machismo no doubt kept him from referring to her for any questions.

A week ago Guy would never have imagined moving out of his apartment so soon after his relocation to Los Angeles with Rose.

But it's time to grow up and put the past behind me, Guy thought. *No more tiny apartments. No more crappy jobs. Time to get serious.* After his first week at MGM he knew things were looking up. Guy believed that some time at an established studio, even if it was just running papers from office to office and picking up the daily triple skim chai latte for his boss, was a step forward. It was time to give Rose the life he had promised her. It was time for Guy to work toward his own dreams of writing the next great script for Hollywood.

Guy looked to his right—Rose was attempting to give the workers some instruction via pantomime and popping sounds— then to his left: an empty fishbowl with a bit of algae crusted inside. He opened another Bud.

Carl hoisted Guy into his apartment. They had been drinking heavily and chatting about Guy's troubles with his wife. He had been several days late with the rent over the past two months but Carl was a sympathetic building manager and joined Guy for a few beers to console him and to try to understand him. They had made a habit of going on morning and evening jogs together, so going out for a few beers afterward wasn't a big deal.

Rose was visiting family back home to get some clarity on their situation, so Carl just let himself in. He could tell the TV was on. White noise buzzed in his ears. With one of Guy's arms over his shoulders Carl helped him into his bedroom. Guy, twenty-six and pretty trim, proved to be quite difficult for Carl to drag around. His apartment was located directly above Carl's, so the layout was exactly the same. This gave Carl some advantage, as the space was pitch-black. In the bedroom he plopped Guy onto the queen-sized frame. The curtains were open, letting the full moon shine in.

Rose had been quite insistent on each room having its own theme. The bedroom was the ocean floor. She found a variety of sheet sets with tropical fish patterns that she adored and sought out appropriate accents for the rest of the room. Rotating beach-scene lamps, porcelain fish and seashell wall pieces, even a small fishbowl on the nightstand with 3 round goldfish sloshing about. She'd even gone as far as painting the walls a deep aqua blue.

"Why does the bedroom have to look like this? I feel like I'm just another one of your fat fish."

"You're not fat, honey."

"You know what I mean. Why not decorate the bathroom with all this crap? Seems a little more fitting if you ask me." Guy fiddled with a starfish on the wall that appeared to be winking at him.

"Careful with that," Rose tapped at Guy's chest and read-justed the fish before going back to making the bed. *"But aren't these sheets darling?"*

"They're neon pink," Guy sighed. *"I just don't get the angel-fish hat-and-cane shtick. It's stupid."*

Rose pouted. *"Why do you always have to be so negative? Can't you have just a little fun?"*

"I just think they're tacky is all, but what do I know? I'm just a guy," he said, defeated.

"That's right, dear. You're just the man," she teased. *"Now get out there and make some money so I can turn the living room into a zoo!"*

Carl was set to draw the shades when he caught a glimpse of Guy on the bed. The moon beamed against the red curtains

making the room breathe deep mauve. It had the look of an
aquarium on acid gone mad and Guy was in the center of it.
Slopped on the edge of the bed with his arms stretched across,
his midriff was exposed. No wonder Carl had such a time
getting him home. Guy was small indeed but had a toned,
athletic frame. Carl had never noticed this before. Guy always
bundled himself in baggy sweatpants and a hoodie when they'd
go jogging together. Carl sat himself next to his sauced friend.
His unyielding stomach rose and fell with fluidity. The faint
downy hairs that covered his entire torso glistened like stardust
in the moonlight. Carl placed his hand on Guy's stomach and
immediately pulled away. The flesh, warm, made him panic.
Carl realized it was time for him to get into his own bed. It
was late and he had had just about one drink too many and his
drunk was getting the best of him.

"That's all right," Guy whispered, as Carl got back up to
draw the curtains.

"What?" Carl said keeping his gaze at the moon. He was
flushed with an adolescent frenzy.

"I said"—Guy kicked his feet onto the bed—"it's all right if
you wanna touch me."

Carl heard the unmistakable sound of an unzipping fly. He
squeezed his eyes tight. His heart raced, but he managed to turn
back and look at Guy. He was lying on the center of the bed
with his pants undone, looking directly at Carl. One hand was
tucked behind his head and the other just beneath his Fruit of
the Looms. His trench coat splaying to either side made him
look like Nosferatu gone nubile in a deep-sea adventure. This
eerie combination with the surge in his own pants was all too
much for Carl. His panic only increased.

"You're drunk. You don't know what you're saying," Carl
rationalized. "You go to sleep. I'll see you tomorrow for a run."

He quickly closed the curtains and made his way through the dark to his own apartment. He needed to forget about the psychotic sea he'd been wading in and wake up to a bright new day.

Carl was on his knees in the courtyard getting bloody knuckled working on a weed that had rooted itself underneath a stone bench. His father, a Mexican immigrant, had told him it was always best to use your hands. Tools only complicated things. Even as a kid he knew his dad was full of it. He knew it had everything to do with his family being poor. Carl was no longer living in the small Korea town studio with his mom, dad and three sisters. He was managing a twenty-four-unit building in Hollywood, so at the ripe age of forty-three he could easily shell out some cash for gardening tools to make his job easier, and he had. Getting up, he wiped the beads of sweat from his forehead on the handkerchief he always had in his back pocket. He was headed for the tool shed he had built in the corner of the courtyard when Guy whizzed by hitting him on the shoulder. He seemed frazzled.

"Out of hiding, I see." Carl chuckled and leaned down to pick up the handkerchief that had fallen. He hadn't seen Guy in over a week.

"I'm on my way to my new job. I'm already late," Guy said coldly, making it clear he had no intention of chatting. "I have the rent upstairs. Meet me at my apartment at seven tonight and I'll have it for you then. I gotta run."

"Oh, okay," Carl said, folding up the handkerchief. "I'll just give a knock on your door then." He watched Guy zoom out and wondered if he had actually found a new job or even if he'd ever see him again. Guy seemed cold. Carl wanted to stay calm, but he could feel something inside him grow as Guy disappeared from sight. He wished he'd never touched his stomach that night. He wished he'd never joined him for a drink in the first place. He wished he'd just kept to himself rather than complicating other people's already complicated lives. Then he wished he'd done just as Guy asked: continued touching him and stayed with him that night.

Carl was in his living room polishing off some Manuel Puig when he heard Guy come home. The red digital on the clock tucked into his bookcase flashed 7:27 PM. He continued reading to give Guy some time to settle in before going up to collect the rent. After a few minutes of shuffling sounds and heavy footsteps, it was silent. Carl put his book down and dug his feet into his slippers that were tucked neatly beneath the sofa. He had a brief moment of panic before realizing his keys were by the front door in the glass ashtray he used for excess change on the small table. Then he realized he was in a pair of faded gray sweatpants and a long-sleeved thermal shirt that had been stained with bleach.

Perhaps I should change? Silly old man, he thought.

Guy opened the door as soon as Carl arrived.

"So, the rent." He stepped aside and invited Carl in. "Want some tea?

Tea? Carl thought. "Sure. What do you have?"

"Not sure, really. Whatever Rose bought." Guy headed to the kitchen and rummaged through the cupboard.

"Congratulations on the job, Guy." Carl sat down at the mini diner-style table by the window. The summertime dusk grazed his elbow as he fiddled with the pink doily on the center of the table.

"I've been working on cutting back on beer. Trying to be a little more focused and responsible. You know? Rose and I have been talking. She's still out of town, which has been good for us.

I think. Some time to think, you know?" Guy was pulling boxes of tea from the cupboard and placing them on the counter. "Anyhow, things seem to be getting better but who knows for how long? Things could go to hell when she gets back on Friday but I'm feeling hopeful. I have a job now. I'm not drinking. Things could be real good for us."

Friday was in two days. "That's very good to hear, Guy."

"Is it?" Guy sounded shocked by Carl's response.

"What's that supposed to mean?"

"Nothing. I just thought—"

"Careful!" Carl quickly got up from his seat.

Guy over poured boiling water into the teapot that now was making its way over the counter and onto his hand. He dropped the kettle onto the floor.

"Shit!" Guy fiercely shook his hand.

"Put it under cold water." Carl moved in and turned on the tap. He grabbed hold of Guy's hand with both of his and let the cold water run over their intermingled fingers. Guy's heavy breathing came over Carl's neck.

"That does feel good." Guy was now resting his chin on Carl's shoulder.

"You have some sugar?" Carl asked.

"Sugar?"

"I take mine with cream and sugar." Carl pulled himself away and put the kettle back on the stove. To wipe up the excess water from the floor and counter he used a pink dishtowel with bold red letters in cursive that read "Hers" that was hanging from the oven handle.

"Sure." Guy went to turn off the faucet.

"No! Keep it under for another minute," Carl insisted, holding Guy's hand again with his.

"It's in this cabinet." Guy pointed with a slight cock of his neck to the cupboard they both were facing. Carl reached up to open the cabinet. He felt Guy's nose graze his underarm. Jostled, he pulled away with the sugar in hand.

Face-to-face, Guy went for it. He pulled Carl in close by his waist.

Without any time to react, Carl just kissed Guy back with the same intensity that was being given to him. The tap rushed and the glass sugar jar exploded as Carl's hands grasped onto Guy's shoulder blades.

He lifted Carl onto the countertop, knocking off the teapot, cups and already soiled boxes of tea and spice jars that rested on it. He shoved his hands underneath Carl's shirt and squeezed him close.

"Man, you smell good."

Carl had no response. He had been working in the yard all day and his aroma was proof of that.

Guy ripped off Carl's shirt and threw it across the room. It landed on the table, knocking the doily onto the floor to be covered sticky with water, sugar crystals, spices and slivered glass. Guy lifted Carl's arms over his head and held him in place by his wrists. He went from his lips and made his way down to his chin, then his neck and then his armpits.

Carl struggled as Guy chewed down, and attempted to break free, but Guy was adamant. He had never had a man gorge himself on his stench before, and here he was, shirtless, in a mess of a kitchen that smelled like hot sticky buns and perspiration, with his male tenant's face in his armpits. He felt dirty. It felt good.

Between his legs, Guy held Carl in place and moved his hands to his upper thighs while Carl pressed the tips of his feet onto the stove and woodblock just behind Guy.

His slippers were glued to the glazed linoleum but he didn't care. He actually didn't have a care for anything in the world at that particular moment. He just knew he felt good and decided to stay there. Carl pushed himself into Guy's hands, which had managed to roll down the waistband of his sweatpants just above crotch level.

"What about you?" Carl said, as Guy buried his face in his groin and took a deep whiff, musky and fragrant: *Suavitel* with the patent smell of man.

"Don't rush things." Guy paused, resting his chin on Carl's swelling lap. "Fair is fair though, right?" He unbuttoned his Ralph Lauren knockoff and tossed it aside onto Carl's thermal. He definitely spent some time at the gym. His pectorals, firm, sported perky pink nipples. His entire torso was just as firm as his chest and his stomach was just as smooth as Carl remembered. Carl suddenly felt self-conscious about his own body. Though he maintained a well-balanced diet and went on those morning jogs to the Observatory he was approaching his midforties. His body could only do so much. He was stocky and round in the gut and that was that. No matter how well he took care of his body, his age, in a way, would define him. This, and the sparse and erratic hair on his chest, had him shying away but marveling at Guy's perfect physique.

"You are so beautiful." Carl placed his hands on Guy's stomach. He bushed his thumbs up and down some of the only substantial hair on his frame, a tuft of blondish fuzz just below his naval.

"So are you, Mister Gutierrez," Guy teased, and gave Carl a light punch on his chest before kissing him and removing his sweatpants altogether.

"That's it!" Rose put her empty cup on the pavement and skipped toward the U-Haul.

The clapping sound of her neon-green flip-flops against her heels was a reminder of what Guy's life was like before moving to L.A. Life when things were far simpler for the two of them. Love didn't even matter. They were young and life was fun. Nothing was concrete and everything was possible. He was reminded of the life before he had any thought of being "something."

He was an avid fan of the films from the New Hollywood era. He was determined to write something as fresh and ground-breaking as Larry McMurtry's *The Last Picture Show* or Paddy Chayefsky's *Network*. These were the true geniuses of the Hollywood that was now dead, and Guy considered himself an expert on the subject. He only hoped he could make his mark on what Hollywood could be again. He had landed a few jobs, mostly TV commercials, editing a few music videos, but nothing he considered worthwhile.

Guy tried to think back to the time when he was in love with Rose, but he couldn't. He knew he had love for her, but even with the setting sun making her auburn hair glisten against her fair skin and her emerald eyes, he couldn't bring himself back to that place. He wondered if he ever had been *in* love with her.

Rose paid the Mexicans fifteen dollars apiece and offered each a Popsicle of his choice.

"I have strawberry and orange. You boys must be hot; I know I am and all I've done is hang out with this guy." She nudged Guy on the shoulder and rummaged through the cooler. Each of the men was wiping away sweat by stretching the bottom of their already drenched T-shirts to the tops of their shiny foreheads. Neither of them wanted a Popsicle, however. Only one was bold enough to ask for a beer—the alpha of course. He sort of bowed his head in a patient dog-like fashion. He rolled the bottom of his stretched-out shirt with his fists giving Guy a good look at his full but firm stomach. His heavy eyebrows blocked the sun from his dark brown eyes that were fixed on Guy. The other three waited patiently just behind him.

"Is that all right, honey?" Rose asked.

Without a word Guy got up from the stoop and brushed her away. She started collecting the beer cans at her feet like nothing had happened. Guy's newly lit cigarette crackled between his lips. The brave one watched as Guy worked over the remnants of the cooler slowly as if picking the perfect cold beer. Rose ran into the lobby with an armful of crushed cans to throw away. Guy was a little drunk and she could tell, so she took her time inside.

Guy's pants were loose around his waist and tugged on his boxers, revealing much of his behind. A bead of sweat trickled down his back and nestled itself between the soft hairs that covered the top of his crack. The alpha continued to stare and held his breath but said nothing. The other three's attention was on the cooler. After picking that perfect Bud, Guy quickly turned around with a charismatic smile for his state of drunk.

"Here we go." He handed the Mexican an ice-cold beer.

"*Gracias.*" The worker reached for it but with his sweaty palms and the melted ice on the can, it slipped through his fingers. Guy caught it before it hit the ground and handed it back to him. Distracted by his dark eyes, Guy accidentally grazed the worker's crotch with the beer and the back of his hand—just as firm as his stomach and chest appeared to be. The Mexican used both his hands to hold Guy's in place. Guy lazily smiled and just got an acute stare back in return from his newfound friend.

The other three's attention went from Guy to Rose, then from Rose to Guy. *Were these two gringos messing with them?* Not at all. Rose was standing in the entryway of the building with nothing to do but watch, astounded, along with the other workers. She twisted at the loose button on her sweater again until it broke free and bounced down the stairs and onto the hot pavement.

"All right, *mi amigos! Cervesa!*" Guy got up, leaving the beer can in the alpha's hands, and pulling the cigarette from his mouth. He tossed it into the empty fishbowl. "Drink up, it's all yours! Time for me and the missus to head to the new homestead!"

FOOTBALL FUCKBUDDIES

Bearmuffin

Sure, pro football players suck and fuck. Sometimes each other. The NFL would have a fucking cow if they ever knew about me and Bubba Hightower. We were straight as hell, married with kids, but whenever we got together we would fool around.

Bubba is a tall, hulking tackle who has quarterbacks for lunch. His fat cock is mega-sized, with the biggest low-hanging balls I've ever seen in a locker room.

He stands six foot three and weighs 215 pounds. Beetle brows shade his piercing coal-black eyes. His rugged face is angular, fiercely masculine. He's wonderfully V-shaped and has the most spectacular, muscular ass in the world. And a superb set of pecs. A pelt of curly black hair covers his powerhouse body. He looks like a mega-muscled grizzly bear. He's my best fuckbuddy, ever!

I remember the first time we fucked. It was after the Super Bowl. Bubba and I returned to our hotel. We had won so he wanted to party. Bubba punched me on the shoulder and said, "Let's go for a drink."

I fell on the bed and pulled a pillow over my head.

"C'mon, man," Bubba said. "Let's find some pussy."

"I'm tired, Bubba."

"Hey! What are you? Some kind of fag?"

"Yeah, so what?" I said.

"Huh?" Bubba's eyes were filled with suspicion.

"Just kidding," I said, throwing my hands up defensively.

"Wise guy," he said. "C'mon. Get dressed!"

We went to the hotel bar and ordered drinks. A reporter from a local newspaper was there and we gave him an interview. After he left, two women joined us and introduced themselves. One was blonde, the other brunette. The blonde began fawning over Bubba.

"You're a big guy," she said.

Bubba roared with laughter.

"Wanna see how big?"

Bubba grabbed her hand and pulled it over his crotch. He opened his fly and his semihard cock jutted out. My jaw dropped. His cock was huge and hard, twelve inches of man meat, bigger than any I've seen. When you've been hanging out in a shower room half of your life you get to see plenty of cock, but Bubba's was incredible!

But the sight of all that cock was just too much for the blonde because she screamed and slapped Bubba's face. He responded by throwing his drink at her. I pulled Bubba away before anybody recognized us. The last thing we needed was bad publicity.

But Bubba wanted to party some more so we found another bar. The drunker he got the sloppier he got.

Finally, it was last call. I somehow managed to convince Bubba that we should get back to the hotel. He was stinking drunk. His body odor was powerful, intense, and I had a boner right on the spot. He was a beautiful hairy beast. And I desperately wanted to suck his cock and rim his hairy ass, but he was still semiconscious so I didn't want to fuck around with him.

I tucked Bubba into bed. After a few minutes he fell asleep, his loud snores buzzing through the room. I watched some TV and then dozed off.

The next thing I knew Bubba was on top of me, slapping his big, hard cock against my face.

"Suck it!" he cried. "Suck it! Suck my cock!"

He jammed his cock between my lips, forcing my mouth open as he stuck his cock into my mouth. It wasn't exactly the way I had envisioned blowing Bubba. But what the hell, it was what I'd been wanting to do all night. And if Bubba wanted me to suck his cock, I was more than happy to oblige.

Bubba grabbed my head with both hands as he fed me his big cock. It felt so fucking good inside my mouth. Hot, pulsing and meaty. I responded by sticking my finger up his ass.

Fuck, was I taking a big chance or what? His ass was just swirling with fur. I was jamming my fingers into his butt knuckle-deep. Bubba was moaning and groaning like a stuck pig. I was surprised but happy to see that he loved getting finger-fucked!

I gently slid my finger in and out of his asshole. He pushed his ass back and moaned some more, his anus squeezing around my finger.

"Oh, yeah, buddy!" Bubba cried. "Fuck! That really feels good!"

He glared down at me with a big shit-eating grin on his handsome face. Then he pulled me up and kissed me long and hard, thrusting his tongue deep into my mouth. We fondled each other's muscles as we continued to kiss.

I was trapped underneath his enormous brawn, his huge tree-trunk thighs holding me firm. He hugged me tight, swapping spit with me. It was an incredible experience having this big man on top of me, this huge, hulking brute whimpering and moaning as I kissed him and played with his asshole.

"Suck my cock some more," Bubba said.

I scooted down to his groin. Once again, I took his spectacular cock into my eager mouth. As I sucked him off, Bubba thrust himself forward so that his balls crashed against my chin. They smelled especially raunchy so I was inspired to start sucking on them.

Sucking his balls made him groan even more. Then I returned to sucking on his cock. It was rock hard, throbbing and bobbing, the cock-veins swelling inside my mouth.

The knob of Bubba's cock was huge, like a shiny fat door-knob, glistening with precum. I licked the slit, dipping the tip of my tongue into the dime-sized hole to pull out a thick, silky strand of precum. His jizz tasted warm, salty and rich.

Bubba pushed forward, his cock forcing my jaws wider so that it could hurtle down my aching throat hilt-deep. I was choking on it, gagging to the point of tears.

But I wanted his cock all the way down my throat so I kept it there, clamping my throat muscles firmly around it, jamming the flattened tip of my tongue against the bull-root of his cock. My nose was buried in his dense, curling, musky pubes. The aroma of his groin was spectacular, and I started fisting my cock as I inhaled more of his manly smell.

Bubba tossed his head back in ecstasy. He heaved long, deep sighs. Fuck! Was he ready to shoot his wad? Maybe it was time to give Bubba a good rim job. Yeah, I wondered how he would react to me eating his ass.

I let his cock slip from my mouth. I moved toward his

mammoth thighs and grabbed hold. I found my target again, driving my tongue into his asshole. I felt his buttocks shudder against my probing face. It was crazy how he groaned.

I gave my cock the attention it needed as I ate Bubba out. I knew I was going to cum a big load. It was exciting and so unexpected. Who would have thought that this big butch football stud loved getting rimmed so much?

Then he said something that blew me away.

"I've always wanted to get ass-fucked, but if you tell anybody, I'll break you in two!"

"Not a peep, man."

I smeared some lube on my cock and fingered some on his pucker. He gasped when I touched his hole, which twitched instinctively to my touch.

Bubba lay on his back, propping his big thighs on my shoulders.

"Now go easy, big guy," he said. "This is my first time."

I carefully inserted my cock between his big boulder buttocks while he moaned and whimpered with anticipation. The head of my cock pressed against his sensitive pucker. Bubba gasped and tightened his asshole. But I was ready for that. I had some poppers on hand.

I unscrewed the cap and held the bottle under his nose.

"Here, sniff this."

"What is it?"

"It'll relax you."

Bubba took a long sniff and fell back on the bed dizzy from the fumes. But it did the trick and when my cock was primed and ready to ass-fuck him, his hole was wide and relaxed.

"Fuck me, buddy," he moaned. "Shove your cock up my ass!"

So I went in for the kill.

Bubba bucked and heaved, so I stopped about an inch inside him. Bubba gasped.

I tried to work another inch into his butthole but I felt him tense against me.

"So fucking big!" he cried out.

He grabbed the sides of the mattress as his muscles shuddered against mine.

"Hold on," he moaned, "let me get used it. Your cock is huge!"

I held still, allowing my cock to swell inside his anus. Bubba began pushing back a bit, as his hole opened up wider, letting my meat slowly inch in. I could tell by his moans of pleasure that he was enjoying himself. Yeah, I bet the big lug couldn't wait for me to give him a real ass-pounding.

"Okay, buddy," he said. "Stick it in some more."

I thrust into him again, working my cock another four inches.

Bubba panted some more and told me to hold it there. I could feel my meat swell inside him, throbbing and pulsating.

"Okay," he said, "shove it in."

I resumed plowing into him until my knob banged against his prostate.

Bubba responded with a long, drawn-out cry: "Awww fuuuck!"

I hit the jackpot!

His body went taut. He grabbed my biceps and cried out again. For a moment I thought he would toss me off but he began to relax. That's when I started pumping him a bit and he moaned again. "Yeah, that's good," he said. "Hey, yeah. That feels fucking good."

I gritted my teeth and pumped some more, holding on to his haunches and bringing him back to me.

Bubba really got into the fuck now.

"Fuck harder, stud," he said. "Fuck me harder!"

He really wanted to feel my cock inside him so I pumped him hard, grinding my groin against his meaty butt. My hands flew over his big thick meaty nipples. I tugged and twisted. I ran my tongue along his big bull neck and around his right ear, nibbling on the lobe.

It drove Bubba delirious with lust.

I pumped some more, easing back and then resuming pumping with smooth, even strokes.

"Yeah, fuck me, man. Fuck me!" he cried, pushing his ass back to meet my pumping thrusts.

I felt his tight asshole clutching around my cock, sucking it in deep inside him. I never thought that he'd enjoy getting fucked so much, this big hulking bruiser impaled on my cock.

Bubba began jacking off.

"Shoot your wad, buddy!" he shouted. "Shoot it!"

"You want me to cum, Bubba?"

"Yeah, buddy! Lemme feel your juices inside me!"

That got me so excited, I sank into him to the hilt as my cock erupted, filling his tight hole with cum.

Bubba screamed as he spasmed—"Awww fuuck!"—realizing that he was coming, too. He shrieked and wailed, his cum-spurts shooting all over my belly and pecs, drenching me.

Afterward, he grabbed me, cuddled with me and kissed me again. Yeah, believe it or not, he was a big teddy bear, so soft and gentle. It felt fucking incredible to be wrapped in his big hairy arms. Soon, we both drifted off to sleep.

The next morning Bubba got up and showered. He dressed quickly, explaining that he had an appointment to keep. I watched that big grizzly bear amble out the door. I sat there in amazement at what had happened. It took me a while to let it all sink in.

To this day, I don't know much about Bubba's private life outside football other than he's married with kids, but I do know that he loves an occasional ass-fucking—and sometimes even a morning blow job.

So I don't ask any questions.

Why fuck up a good thing? Right?

METAL HEAD

Zeke Mangold

The band was called Tomb of Shadows, from Ontario, Canada, and Dell had fallen in sudden and violent lust with the thin lead vocalist, nineteen, beautiful even if he was engulfed in dense fog. His long, straight, blond hair and tight leather pants. His evil black-and-white makeup meant to intensify an image of inhumanity. His Gibson Flying V guitar, wielded like an arrow-shaped, strap-on phallus. His mascara-rimmed blue eyes. The music was life-denying, sex-denying, but the singer—*shrieker*, actually—couldn't thwart Dell's gaydar. Beer would make things go easier.

Tomb of Shadows encored with yet another anti-Christian anthem, "Guillotine the Sheep," before the lights and house music came up. Since the band headlined, there was no need to tear down gear. The band members simply walked off the stage, navigated through the small crowd, and bellied up, eager to cash in their few remaining drink tickets. Dell intercepted the singer, the last one to reach the bar.

"I'm Dell," he said, shaking the musician's black-nail-polished hand. It was soft, but the grip was firm. "Big Tomb of Shadows fan now."

"Hey, thanks. Name's Crighton. Nice to meet you."

"Let me buy you a real Canadian brew. Molson?"

Crighton laughed, shook his head. "Actually, that's a Coors product. But sure."

Dell smiled. He got the bartender's attention, paid cash for two beers and handed Crighton a bottle. Dell encouraged him to clink a toast.

"Great set."

"It was okay," shrugged Crighton.

"I'd treat you to some poutine, but Vegas doesn't serve it."

"Ha. Not a fan. Gravy makes me gag."

Dell imagined what else might cause him to choke.

"Been to Canada, have you?" asked Crighton.

"My mom's a professor. She took me to academic conferences in Toronto, Vancouver and Montreal. Montreal's where I first had poutine."

Crighton nodded, then glanced at the stage. "I'd better get my stuff out of here. Some of these kids might have sticky fingers."

"Let me carry something."

"Cool, thanks."

Dell lugged the amplifier head while Crighton pushed the wheeled speaker cabinet across the parking lot. Dell made eye contact with a woman in a push-up bra, fishnets and heels, smoking a cigarette. She put it out, smiled at Dell and went inside.

It was Shelly, drummer for The Dildogs and an online porn company office admin, who'd turned him on to the extreme musical subgenre of black metal. For a while, Dell had shared a bed with the older president of said adult site, Bait Box, but the relationship fizzled out, and the young Las Vegan found himself spending more time with Shelly. She'd helped line him up with a job selling insurance to Mexican food truck operators and accompanied him as his guide into the realm of underground rock. Shelly was also the best wing woman on the planet.

Crighton opened the van's rear door and stood to one side of the cabinet. "Little help?"

Dell heaved the amp next to the wheel well and grabbed a handle on the cab. Together they lifted the heavy speaker into the van. Crighton was inside when Dell jumped in, closed the van door and kissed the metal head on the lips.

"Hey, wait a second. I'm not gay," he said weakly.

"I know," said Dell. He kissed Crighton again.

"My band's bringing their gear now."

"No. They're distracted."

"By whom?"

"My friend Shelly."

"The blonde in the fishnets? I saw you look at her. Dell and Shell."

"Enough about her. Take off your pants."

"I told you—"

"Relax. I'm not going to ass-fuck you. I'm just swallowing your cum."

Dell noticed Crighton visibly shudder with anticipation before lying down in the back of the van, undoing his bullet belt and removing his black T-shirt.

The musky odor of the metal head's hairy, sweaty balls hit Dell's nostrils and he felt his cock straining against his jeans. He crawled over to Crighton and quickly took the long, hard, uncircumcised, precum-dripping shaft in his hands. He began to fondle Crighton's testicles and stroke his erection.

His pierced left nipple between Dell's lips, Crighton spread his legs, leather pants still snaring his ankles, and whispered, "Eat my asshole."

Dell stuck his tongue deep into the metal head's crack and heard a growl of pleasure.

Still, he couldn't wait to get his mouth on Crighton's dick. He sensed the so-called straight boy's hips push into him as he engulfed the head of the penis in his mouth. Dell sucked it brilliantly. He'd learned how to relax his gag reflex. He took the whole shaft, right down to the sac. He'd never been able to do that before.

In mere seconds, Crighton filled Dell's mouth with hot, spurting jizz. The young insurance salesman hungrily swallowed every last drop. Clearly it had been some time since Crighton had enjoyed a release, because his semen was thick, voluminous.

"Drink it, bitch," Crighton snarled.

Dell handled it like a pro. After sipping the last drops of joy juice from the piss slit, he looked up at Crighton and licked his lips. Crighton's eyes were closed, but he had a big grin on his face. Dell squeezed the now-shrinking cock and put it back in the metal head's pants, zipped them up and buckled the bullet belt.

Now that he was more or less reclothed, Crighton looked embarrassed. He stood up clumsily, banging his head on the van's ceiling, and pulled the black T-shirt over his skinny frame. He cleared his throat. Dell, meanwhile, remained hypnotized by the musician's staggering beauty. At twenty-three, he felt like the older man in this scenario.

"Um," said Crighton.

"Yes?" said Dell.

The metal head licked his thumb to wipe a spot of hellish makeup from Dell's cheek. Dell was in heaven.

"We're playing Flagstaff, Arizona, tomorrow," said Crighton. "You could maybe drive out and see us? It's only, like, a two-hour drive."

"Sounds good. I'll be there."

"Really? Great."

Crighton unlatched the van door and swung it open. No one was in the parking lot; his band was still inside the bar, likely flirting with Shelly, the perfect honey trap.

They went back inside, acting as if nothing had happened. Dell was fine with that. He would have another shot at Tomb of Shadows' front man in twenty-four hours in the neighboring Grand Canyon State. Meantime, he bought the whole band—plus his gorgeously effective wing woman—a round of Sierra Nevada Pale Ales.

"Vegas beer?" asked Crighton, studying the label on the bottle.

"Actually, it's a California product," said Dell, grinning.

After they'd spent hours of copious drinking and many last calls, the bar finally kicked them out.

"I thought Sin City never closed," said Crighton, stumbling into the parking lot.

"A myth," said Dell. "Everything that lives must eventually die, including Vegas bars."

"What's your cell? I'll text you my number."

Dell recited it and felt his phone vibrate when Crighton messaged him. He wanted to place the phone directly on the metal head's prostate, massaging it until climax.

Drunk, the band piled into the van, pizza boxes and empty beer cans spilling out.

"Smells like ass in here," said the drummer.

"Smells like one of your cum rags," cracked the guitarist.

Mortified, Dell and Crighton quickly shook hands, then

awkwardly waved good-bye to each other.

When Dell got into Shelly's car, she said, "And?"

"And nothing."

"His cum tastes like...?"

"Pure salt. I need water."

She handed him a warm Fiji, which he gulped.

"The drummer," she said, turning the ignition key. "He has large, rough hands. I want him to hold me down with those meat hooks as he brutally stabs me from behind."

"I prefer turning out straight boys. With soft, dainty mitts."

"How straight can he be? That's a lot of makeup he's wearing."

"It's black metal. Part of the whole dark and evil vibe."

"Oh, so *you're* the expert on underground music now?"

"No, just on the proper and improper application of mascara."

They both laughed at that.

The Vegas bars that hosted black-metal gatherings were a bit on the—how to put it delicately?—*shitty* side, with bartenders slinging coke and meth to make up for meager tips provided by blue-collar construction types, most of whom ordered Buds and remained unemployed in a distressed economy that just a few years earlier had boomed with no end in sight. There was something about the surface nihilism of black metal, its kabuki-grade theatricality, that attracted Dell during the brutal summer of 2011, when Wall Street coughed like an ancient, emphysema-stricken whore as Dell's vapid coworkers soothed the pain of watching their 401k's turn into dust by chatting in the break room about "Jersey Shore." Dell wasn't a nihilist, not even close, yet at twenty-three he was beginning to wonder this: like, the point of it all?

He treated his angst and deranged his senses à la Rimbaud with high-volume performances by national touring acts from as far away as Italy, England and the Netherlands. But no matter from where these black-metal bands traveled, they always based their stage presence on the Scandinavian tradition of corpse paint, spiked armbands, bullet belts and inverted crosses. Dell had always looked upon satanic heavy metal as being deeply misanthropic and vaguely aligned with National Socialism—and a very small percentage of this music was, in fact, this way. But after inspecting the music more closely, Dell saw it for what it was—a ceremonious protest by the alienated individual against the drone-like masses. In other words, dirty fun.

Dell had long been a practitioner of dirty fun. A scholar of it, in fact.

"Come with me to Flagstaff," he blurted out to Shelly as he made her French toast in his kitchen. Not wanting to risk a DUI, she'd slept in the guest bedroom.

Smiling, she stirred Splenda in her coffee. "Wow. Must be serious."

"No. It never is."

"Uh-huh. So when's the last time you left the city limits for a piece of ass?"

Dell had to think about this. He drew a blank and almost burned the toast.

"What's that?" said Shelly.

"You know, I love cooking breakfast for a bitchy girl who isn't wearing any panties."

Shelly groaned, pulling her GG Allin T-shirt over her exposed, waxed crotch. "God, you make me sound like Britney Spears. I just don't like wearing them with that skirt for some reason. I can't explain it."

Dell raised his hand, ending that line of conversation. "I need my wing woman."

"Why not take your other hag, London?"

"She hates loud guitars. Your familiarity with the music emboldens me."

"So now you're using me to fuck not-so-straight metal heads?"

Dell quietly sprinkled cinnamon and placed the final product on the table in front of Shelly. "Bon appétit," he added.

"I'll say the same, since I'm going with you to Arizona so you can munch Crighton's cock. But you drive and I get to choose the music the entire way there—and back!"

"Can I import Tomb of Darkness into your iPod?"

"One song," she said, shoving a forkful of French toast into her mouth. "Mmm. Pass the syrup? Thanks. Oh, and you have to attend our next rehearsal. No excuses."

Shelly had been encouraging Dell to become the new lead vocalist for The Dildogs, who'd just lost their singer to a crippling ear infection. Dell thought he lacked the confidence necessary to stand in front of a microphone onstage, but in fact he'd written lyrics for a few songs that he was secretly dying to show Shelly.

"Will do," he said. "It'll be good to see a black metal show in another city."

They took Route 66 to Flagstaff, a four-hour drive, and nearly killed each other when Dell insisted on popping in a W.A.S.P. CD, *The Last Command*, which Shelly loathed because it reminded her of a jerky ex-boyfriend. But Dell really wanted to hear "Ball Crusher" and "Jack Action," comic-book tales of sexual revenge. They made him laugh, though they frightened him. He was singing along to "Wild Child" when Shelly (Dell's car had a flat tire) turned off the music and took her foot off the accelerator.

"What's up?"

"Oh, my god, look," she said. "They broke down!"

"Who?"

"The band! Tomb of Shadows."

"What?"

Sure enough, there on the side of the road was the very van in which Dell had blown Crighton, steam now rising from the radiator. Crighton and his band stood in front of the battered vehicle, staring down at the engine, the open hood propped open thanks to the drummer's hi-hat stand. The musicians exuded a collective sense of confusion and frustration, as if they were unable to decide whether to call an expensive tow company or to don hiking shoes. The nearest exit was miles away.

Shelly coasted into the breakdown lane and parked behind the van.

"Oh, hey," said Crighton, smiling at Dell's arrival. "Know anything about cars?"

"I do, actually." As Dell walked to the front of van, the band members parted to make room for him. The steam mostly dissipated, he inspected the radiator for a moment.

"It's coming from this rubber hose," he said, jiggling the offending tube. "I've got a quick fix. Got duct tape somewhere?"

"We do," said Crighton. "Billy?"

The drummer retrieved a roll of duct tape from the back of the van, handing it to Dell. Dell dried the hose with a dirty towel someone had left on the bumper, tore off a three-inch piece of duct tape, and placed it over the hole in the radiator hose, pressing the tape firmly in place. Then he tore off a longer piece and, starting two inches above the smaller piece of tape, wrapped it around and around the hose tightly, pressing it into place. Next, he checked the radiator fluid level.

"You have enough to reach Flagstaff. To be safe, I'm adding plain old water."

With that, Dell cracked open a Dasani and poured it in.

"Holy shit, thanks," said Crighton. "My dad's a mechanic, but I never paid attention. He's always drunk anyway."

"I was raised by a single mom," explained Dell. "I had to learn to do everything. I was pumping her damn gas at five."

"Ha!" Crighton patted Dell's back. "All right, we're running late and need to move. See you at the club, guys."

"No problem. We'll follow you there."

"Thanks again!"

An hour later, they pulled up to the tavern, Squiggy's, near the railroad tracks. Tomb of Shadows began unloading equipment—drum kit, amps, guitar cases. Dell and Shelly went inside to drink Coronas and commandeer the Internet jukebox, watching as the band dragged their gear onstage and conducted an eardrum-lacerating sound check. The song "Inverted Crosshairs" seemed particularly inspired.

It was at this point that Dell felt a lump in his throat. Turned out Crighton had a Flagstaff groupie, a young frat-looking college guy trying to compensate with cargo shorts, MMA shirt, and backward baseball cap. He was hanging around the black-metal front man, too close for Dell's taste, and trying to chat up the musician. Worse, it seemed to be working; Crighton smiled, laughed and nodded his head. It hurt Dell.

Shelly noticed his defeated attitude. "Pangs of jealousy?" she said.

Dell shrugged, swigged from his Corona.

Eventually, everyone ended up in the backstage dressing room, eating peanut M&M's and waiting for the 10:00 p.m.

show to start. There were two opening bands, both from
Arizona, the members of whom talked incessantly about getting
high and from whom to buy the weed. The exchanges tended to
go like this:

"Dude, no! Amanda's the shit. She sold me a quad of leafy
dank for, like, forty bucks. You can't beat that, dude!"

"No, dude. I know this one guy with a dub of Purple Kush.
Let's go to *his* place!"

"Forget all that, dude. Chronic Chris lives just a mile down
the road, yo!"

The debate spilled out into the hallway, as the bands and an
inebriated Shelly began making their way to the ideal purveyor
of psychoactive bliss and a halfway decent pizza joint with which
to soak up all the booze in their systems. Dell found himself
alone in the dressing room with Crighton and the groupie.

"Lock the door," said Crighton.

Dell felt his heart skip a beat, but did as he was told. He
walked over and turned the latch. He made eye contact with
the groupie, who quickly looked down at his shoes. He avoided
Dell's gaze at first, acting as if he was unsure he wanted to go
through with what was obviously taking place. As if!

"Don't move, Dell," Crighton said.

With a piece of white chalk, he squatted on the ground to
etch a pentagram—or the five-pointed star—on the dressing-
room carpet. He ordered the groupie to strip and lie down on
the floor, on his back, and to spread his arms and legs inside the
chalk-marked pentagram. The groupie obeyed, revealing black
thong underwear.

"Take that off, too," said the metal head as he lit incense and
a few fat white candles.

The groupie removed the thong and, lying on the carpet,
spread his limbs like Leonard Da Vinci's *Virtuvian Man*. Dell

could see he was already erect, a solid eight inches, hairless. The perfect frat-guy body with a smidgen of beer-drinking fat.

Crighton removed his own shirt and pants and dimmed the dressing-room lights.

Suddenly the room was silent, except for some soft sucking and kissing noises. Crighton was down on one knee, stooping to kiss the groupie on the mouth and on the cock. Dell was incredibly aroused; his own shaft was throbbing.

Crighton uttered the words "Aeh Do'oh N'yay." The Wiccan phrase startled Dell, making him think he'd stepped into some dark satanic rite that he would regret later—not for its obvious sexual content but for its latent violence.

The groupie's cock was larger than Dell's. Crighton's big, pouty lips were wrapped tightly around it; he deep-throated it, bobbing his head up and down, rubbing the groupie's abs as he sucked. Dell was envious of the groupie's superior physique.

The frat boy let out an animalistic moan, a *begging* moan, and got up on his hands and knees, haunches in the air. One of his hands reached back toward his ass as he tried to find Crighton's dick. The metal head was already beating off, stroking it desperately. The groupie pulled the black-metal sausage toward his asshole, so Crighton spit right in the frat boy's ass-crack, for lubrication.

Dell could see the groupie wince as Crighton started to go inside him. The groupie looked like he was having fun, but also like he'd done this before.

"Come in my asshole, please," he said, panting, a mischievous grin on his face. "I want you *both* to come inside my butt."

Dell couldn't believe his ears. He watched as the groupie pushed his hips into Crighton's thrusting, taking every inch of the metal head's veiny cock. Crighton's eyes were closed; he bit his lower lip and started moaning with each stroke.

"Crighton," said the groupie, "I want your load. Shoot it."

He did just that, cramming his cock all the way to the hilt inside the frat boy's pink asshole, coming deep inside.

"Your turn," he said to Dell, gasping for breath even as he stood up, jizz still leaking from the tip of his dong.

"Did you douche?" Dell asked the groupie, whose tight butt-hole was dripping cum.

"Always, yes," he replied. "Please use my ass!"

"Give me second." Dell got on his knees in front of Crighton and cleaned off his dick, which tasted of saline and lube and semen, and licked his ashy balls.

Then he dropped his own jeans and prepared to doggy-style the frat boy.

"Listen, you," growled Dell. "I'm going to come in your mouth, not in your ass, and you're going to swallow every drop and love it."

"Yes! Come in my mouth!"

Dell put his hand on his neck and thrust into him, pumping fast and furious.

"Your balls are slapping mine," said the groupie, who whimpered as the pressure on his prostate caused him to ejaculate, watery sperm spraying the carpet.

Crighton, still buck-naked, jumped in, catching some of it with his hand and eating it, then kissing the groupie so he could get a taste of his own sauce.

This was too much. Dell increased his strokes and tightened his fingers around the groupie's neck as he usually did before he came. When he was close, he stood up and circled to the groupie's front and started stabbing his mouth.

"Oh, god," bellowed Dell, ramming himself in one last time, holding it there for a few moments as he spurted his joy juice down the groupie's hot wet throat before collapsing on top of him. The frat boy gurgled contentedly as Crighton kissed him on the mouth, flickering candlelight casting eerie shadows on the walls.

After the show, as Tomb of Shadows' final power chords ripped through the dry Southwestern night, Dell practically pushed Shelly out of the club, into the parking lot and onto the steering wheel of her car.

"Hey, what's the rush? I thought you were in lust."

"Well, yes. But he's a *real* Satanist."

"Real as in for real? Ritual abuse and everything?"

"Something like that. We fucked each other—and the frat boy—inside a pentagram."

"The symbol in the dressing room? I thought it looked weird."

"It was fun, but a little too spooky."

"So-called straight guys can get a little weird. Where to?"

"Vegas. I need to be surrounded by my people."

"Your people are Martians."

Dell laughed. This time he manned up and drove the whole way back.

ON A PLANE

Shane Allison

When Chris told me at Applebee's that he was taking Ciara with him to Atlantic City, I damn near choked on my mozzarella cheese sticks. Her. His so-called girlfriend who didn't bother to visit him the entire six months he was in jail. I mean I only went to see him every day, waiting in visitation for two hours just to talk to him for a bullshit thirty minutes, and now he was taking that bitch that wouldn't piss on him if he was on fire. Needless to say, I lost my appetite for the turkey bacon burger and the fries I had ordered. That's what I get for wearing my heart on my sleeve: a steak knife clean damn through it.

"So when you thinkin' 'bout goin'?" I asked.

"Probably in a week or two. I need to call Ciara and tell 'er."

"You haven't told 'er yet?"

"My folks just gave me the tickets today."

I eavesdropped on Chris breaking the news to Ms. Hood Rat.

"Hey, guess what?" I looked at him with a fake expression of excitement as he broke the news to her. I could hear her muffled bouts of glee reverberating from his cell.

"Yeah, whenever you wanna go."

"Love you too," Chris said. I wanted to throw up in my mouth. I picked at my food, pushing shoestring French fries across my sandwich plate.

"What's wrong wit'choo? You ain't hungry?" Chris asked.

"They put too much mustard on my sandwich. I told her light mustard."

"Then send it back," said Chris.

"It's fine. I'll just wipe it off." I took a few napkins and dabbed the excess mustard off the turkey.

"I'd send that shit back if I was you."

I didn't give two shits about no damn sandwich. As far as I was concerned, dinner had gone south. Once again, Ciara: 1, me, 0.

"You want the rest of your fries?"

"Go 'head." Chris reached over and took my plate, scraping my fries onto his own.

"Can you do me a favor? Can you feed and walk Lucky while I'm gone?" I watched as he drowned *his* fries in ketchup.

"Yeah, I guess." The bubbly waitress returned with a pitcher of beer.

"Can I get you guys anything else? Refill on your drinks?"

"No, we good," I said.

"Okay, well, have a good night and come back and see us." She laid the check on the table. Chris paid for dinner and left the waitress a five-buck tip.

We stood talking in the lot of the restaurant. "You work tomorrow?" I asked.

"Nine t' six, then I gotta bowl, but I'll call ya." I put on my best fake smile and said, "I should be aroun'." We got into our cars and drove off in separate directions.

As soon as I got on the road good, I punched the dashboard with a fistful of anger. "After all I did for him. I cain't believe he takin' that ho t' Atlantic City."

That night I didn't sleep worth a damn with Chris on the brain. I had to think of something to stop him from taking Ciara with him to Atlantic City. My last plan kept her so pissed with Chris, it kept him in the doghouse for weeks. I left a Valentine's Day card, unsigned, on the windshield of his car. He called me full of piss and vinegar about how she came up to borrow the car and found the card, asking him who was giving him cards. She thought for sure it was another bitch 'cause of my girlish penmanship. 'Course Chris was forgiven as soon as her ass needed rent money.

My plan had to pack a wallop. I'm talking some "Dynasty," Alexis Carrington kind of shit. After tossing and turning all night, I had an idea. I gave my homegirl, Shareeka, who worked as an escort at Sugar and Spice, a call. I told her about my plan.

"You still messin' 'round wit that same guy? Won'tchoo leave 'im alone?" she said.

"You go'n do it or what?"

"You still owe me a hundred dollars from that shit you pulled th' las' time."

"I'll double it if you do me this favor."

"I want my fuckin' money up front, an' no IOU's, nigga."

I told her I would call her the day I wanted it to go down.

The week Chris and Ciara were to leave, Atlantic City was all he talked about.

"Lucky's got enough food, so all you haf t' do is walk 'im three times a day." But I had no intentions of staying behind while those two sauntered down the boardwalk hand in fucking

hand French kissing under the stars. The day before their departure, I was staked out in the lot of Chris's apartment complex.
His PT cruiser was parked. I called the bowling alley. One of
his coworkers answered and said he was bowling. Ciara had the
car. I called Shareeka to tell her to meet me at Chris's. When
I saw her coming, I waved her down. She was wearing this
tight number, titties spilling out all over the parking lot. It was
perfect. Bitch knows how to work it.

"You got the money?" I handed her a folded one hundred
dollar bill. Shareeka stuffed it down in her dress, between her
titties.

"You know what to do, right?"

"Knock on the door an' ask if Chris is home."

"Apartment one-oh-five. When you done, meet me at Jimmy
John's."

I sat in a window seat at JJ's looking out for Shareeka. She
finally showed up driving a candy-painted Cadillac.

"So, di'joo do it? Did she say anything t' you?"

"C'mon, man. Pay up," she said.

I pulled the rest of what I owed out of the breast pocket of
my shirt.

"So, wassup?"

"She asked who I was," Shareeka said.

"And what di'joo say?"

"I told her I was his sister."

"His sister? You black, Chris white. Sheen go'n believe that,"
I said.

"Nigga, I did whatchoo told me."

Shareeka's never been the brightest bulb in the bunch. Brain's
in her fucking coochie.

"It don't matta no way. The seed of suspicion has been
planted."

"Well, I would love to sit here and shoot the shit witcho ass, but I got money to make."

"U'mma stick aroun' t' see if Chris'll call."

"You need t' leave that white boy alone an' give Derek a call. He's been askin' about you."

"Tell him U'm off th' market."

I checked my watch. Half past seven. When I got to the bowling alley, Chris was standing outside waiting for Ciara. Bitch was late again. He started walking home. I slowed alongside him and rolled down the window.

"Wassup?" I said.

Chris opened the door and got in.

"Wutton Ciara 'pose t' pick you up?" I asked, knowing good and damn well what had gone down.

"I don't know where her ass is at."

"Di'joo call 'er?"

"She ain't answerin' her cell." When we got to Chris's, his car was in the lot.

"Slow down. I don't want 'er t' see you."

I dropped him off at the set of mailboxes in front of the apartment complex.

"Call me lata," I said.

I drove off in the opposite direction, thinking of her laying into him. Instead of heading home, I took a detour to Borders. As I flipped through several books of travel lit, my cell phone sounded. It was a text message from Chris.

Ciara pissed, it read.

I started to punch in letters. *Y? What happen?*

Chris phoned. I walked off to the bathroom and into a stall for privacy.

My words, *Chris 4 ever,* which I had written on the wall, had not been painted over.

"What she say?"

"Some about a girl lookin' for me, talkin' about she was my sister. I told 'er I don't have a sister."

"Damn, who you think it is?"

"I don't know. She said she was fat with long hair."

Shareeka was fat all right, but that *long* hair of hers was bought from Eve's for $2.99 a bag.

"This ain't one of them girls from Big Kahuna's you be fuckin' wit' is it?"

"No."

"Where Ciara?" I asked.

"Her cousin came to get her."

"Di'joo tell Ciara you ain't know this girl?"

"She thinks I'm lyin'."

"But she goin' witchoo on the trip, right?"

"Guess not. Now my ass is stuck with an extra ticket unless you wanna go."

"What about Luck?"

"I'll put him in the vet 'til I get back."

"Well, ain' no need in wastin' a ticket," I told him.

The next day, we were thirty thousand feet in the air and Ciara's trifling ass couldn't touch him. My plan had worked. Chris and I were on our third cup of vodka when his cell phone chimed. Something I didn't count into the equation. He never goes anywhere without his fucking BlackBerry.

"Who that is?" I asked.

"Ciara," he said.

"What she want?"

"She wants me to call her." Chris dialed her number. I nervously took a sip from my cup. The vodka went warm down my throat.

"It's sayin' no signal." Things were still working in my favor.

I figured I would get rid of his phone somehow once we got to Atlantic City.

"I need t' take a piss," said Chris.

"Need me t' hold it for you?" I joked.

"No."

"C'mon, man. We on a plane. This th' las' place you gotta worry about Ciara."

"Okay, but we gotta be quick."

We sat our liquor in our cup holders. I felt a slight buzz coming on. My mouth watered thinking about my lips around his dick. I looked around to make sure we weren't being watched. The stewardesses were busy pushing trays along the aisle, handing out assorted snacks. I opened the door of the bathroom. Chris was standing at the toilet. Piss pelted in the commode water. I slid my hand under his and held his dick over the mouth of the toilet. I held it still as he peed. I flushed the toilet with my foot. I let down the lid and sat. Chris stood between my legs, his dick erect at my face. It had been a while since I had seen it last. Damn near forgot how big it was. I wrapped my lips around the head of his dick. His hips were narrow, hot in my grip as I sucked. I pulled his shorts and boxers down to his feet.

"Take ya shirt off," I said.

He peeled it off and tossed it on the floor.

The hair I had shaved from his chest was starting to grow back. A thick bed of black pubes tickled my nose.

I rested my hands on his ass as he thrust his dick in my mouth. I could taste precum, slick and salty on my tongue. I thought of Ciara as I went down on her man in an airplane bathroom.

"Play with my balls," he said. I tugged at them with ease as they hung low between his legs. Chris's dick tensed in my mouth. His dick was soaked with my spit when I pulled away.

I stood up, turned around and pulled my jeans down below my thighs. There was only so much room in the bathroom to move around. I assumed the position. My ass was bare to his dick.

"We don't have time for that," he protested.

"Jus' chill. Ween go'n get caught."

I braced myself against the wall. I felt the head of his dick against my ass. Chris parted my booty cheeks and pressed his dick in slowly between them. It didn't take much effort to get it in thanks to the butt plug I often used to keep my hole stretched. Chris hooked his hands over my shoulders as he drilled my ass. It made me remember how good his dick felt inside me. I tried to keep the noise down. Chris held on to my hips as he pushed deeper inside me. I knew he was close the way his maneuvers quickened. Chris pulled out. I didn't want him to. He jacked off over the sink. I took his dick in my possession. I fingered his right nipple. His face turned red in the mirror as he came. We washed up and pulled on our clothes.

"Let's go before someone catches us in here," he said, as he pulled up his shorts, tucking his dick back into the bed of his boxers.

"You go first," said Chris, pulling on his shirt.

I cracked the door just so. All was clear. I walked back to my seat. Chris joined me minutes after.

"You want another drink?" he asked

"I can go for one more." Chris waved down one of the stewardesses.

"Can we get two more vodkas?"

"Sure," she said.

Chris checked his phone to see if Ciara had called.

"What time are we 'posed to get there?"

"I think aroun' eleven thirty, twelve o'clock."

"This shit's go'n be off th' chain," I said.

I couldn't sleep sitting upright, but Chris had nodded off after his last drink. I hijacked the phone from his belt and dropped it in my cup of booze. After letting it soak a bit, I dried it off and gently hooked it back on the leather strap. The next day, the plane landed a little before noon. Chris tried to use his cell as we rode in the cab to the hotel.

"Wha's wrong?"

"My phone's dead," he said.

"It was workin' yesterday. Di'joo charge it up?"

"I think so."

"Don't worry about it. You can do it when we get t' th' hotel." I had a grab bag full of tricks up my sleeve. I was going to make sure that bitch didn't stand in the way of us having a good time.

ABOUT THE EDITOR AND AUTHORS

SHANE ALLISON is the proud editor of over a dozen gay erotica anthologies including *Hot Cops, Backdraft, Brief Encounters: 69 Gay Erotic Shorts, Hard Working Men, Frat Boys* and the Gaybie Award–winning anthology, *College Boys,* to name a few. His stories have graced the pages of seven editions of the critically acclaimed, Lambda Award–winning *Best Gay Erotica,* as well as *Best Black Gay Erotica, Best Gay Bondage Erotica, Bears, Ultimate Gay Erotica, Biker Boys, Surfer Boys* and *Country Boys.* He is the author of *Slut Machine,* a collection of poetry from Queer Mojo. His book-length poetry memoir *I Remember* is forthcoming from Future Tense Books. He is currently working on a new collection of poems and hot new gay erotica anthologies. He is also currently "knocking boots" with a straight friend whose name will remain anonymous.

NICK ARTHUR is a cub from Philadelphia whose day job is being a librarian. He lives with his lover, and spends time gardening, trying to do yoga, traveling to new places and hanging out on a beach a lot like the one in his story. Contact him at nickarthur104@gmail.com.

BEARMUFFIN has written for such gay magazines as *Torso, Mandate* and *Honcho*. His work can now be found in anthologies published by Cleis, Starbooks, Alyson and Bold Strokes. Bearmuffin lives in San Diego and loves to travel in search of grist for his literary mill.

GARLAND CHEFFIELD (garlandserotictales.webs.com) is the pen name of a fulltime actor and writer currently living in Hollywood, who has always had a soft, or is that hard spot, for straight boys. His work has appeared in nearly thirty anthologies including *Homo Thugs, Video Boys, Black Fire, The Sweeter the Juice, Cougars on the Prowl, Sugar and Spice* and others.

HANK EDWARDS is the author of dozens of short stories and several erotic novels, including *Fluffers, Inc., A Carnal Cruise* and *Vancouver Nights*, all featuring his character Charlie Heggensford and available from Lethe. He has also published *Holed Up* and *Destiny's Bastard* through Loose Id. He and his partner live in a suburb of Detroit. Visit his website at hankedwardsbooks.com.

D. FOSTALOVE lives in Smyrna, Georgia, where he is currently at work on several projects, including a follow-up to *Unraveled: Sealed Lips, Clenched Fists*.

JAMIE FREEMAN is a World War II buff with a thing about guys in uniforms and leather. His stories are featured in *Homo Thugs, Beautiful Boys, Black Fire* and *Muscle Men*. He's hard at work on more erotic stories, so stay tuned. Check out his website: jamiefreeman.net.

JEFF FUNK's stories have appeared in *Brief Encounters, Hard Working Men, Skater Boys, Cruise Lines, Hard Hats, My First Time Vol. 5, Ultimate Gay Erotica 2008, Tales of Travelrotica for Gay Men Vol. 2* and *Dorm Porn 2*. He lives in Auburn, Indiana.

BARRY LOWE (barrylowe.net) is the author of the novels *Busting Billy's Butt, The Major and The Miners* and *The Gravy Train*. He writes a weekly sex column for the Sydney glossy free bar rag, *SX*. His sex yarns have appeared in various anthologies as well as eBooks through loveyoudivine Alterotica. His story, "Stocks and Shared," was banned by Amazon.

ZEKE MANGOLD is a Las Vegas blackjack dealer. He survived the 1980 MGM Grand hotel fire by seducing a lifeguard in his parked Trans Am just as smoke began pouring out of the building. As a result, Mangold always trusts his dick.

JEFF MANN has published three books of poetry, *Bones Washed with Wine, On the Tongue* and *Ash*; two collections of personal essays, *Edge* and *Binding the God*; a novella, *Devoured*; a novel, *Fog*; a memoir, *Loving Mountains, Loving Men*; and a volume of short fiction, *A History of Barbed Wire*.

NICK MARENCO lives in Los Angeles, California. His stories have graced the pages of *Handbook Magazine* and *Brief Encounters: 69 Hot Gay Shorts*. Currently, he is in the cinema program at Los Angeles City College where he is developing his prose into film. More of his work can be read at thegapinghole.com.

GREGORY L. NORRIS is the author of *The Q Guide to Buffy the Vampire Slayer* and the forthcoming short and long story collection, *The Fierce and Unforgiving Muse: a Baker's Dozen from the Terrifying Mind of Gregory L. Norris*, among others. Visit him on Facebook or at gregorylnorris.blogspot.com.

ROB ROSEN (www. therobrosen.com), author of *Sparkle: The Queerest Book You'll Ever Love* and *Divas Las Vegas,* has contributed to more than one hundred anthologies, including *Truckers, Best Gay Romance, Hard Hats, Backdraft, Surfer Boys, Bears, Special Forces, College Boys, Biker Boys, Hard Working Men, Afternoon Pleasures, The Handsome Prince, Frat Boys* and *Gay Quickies.*

R. TALENT is a freelance writer who is putting the final touches on his debut novel along with the series he hopes to come from it.

Approximately fifty of **MARK WILDYR's** short stories and novellas exploring developing sexual awareness and intercultural relationships have been acquired by *Freshmen* and *Men* magazines, Alyson, Arsenal, Cleis, Companion, Green Candy, Haworth and STARbooks Press. *Cut Hand,* his full-length historical novel, was published in June of this year. His website is markwildyr.com.

BOB VICKERY (bobvickery.com) has been a regular contributor to various websites and magazines, particularly *Men, Freshmen* and *Inches.* He has five collections of stories published: *Skin Deep, Cock Tales, Cocksure, Play Buddies,* and most recently, *Man Jack,* an audiobook of some of his hottest stories.